Waverly:
A Novel

AMY BELLAMY

Inspired by true events

ISBN-13: 9781792923050

For Jason, with all my love

CONTENTS

"All the world's a stage,

And all the men and women merely players;

They have their exits and their entrances,

And one man in his time plays many parts,"

William Shakespeare (As You Like It, Act II Scene VII)

PART 1

THE CRIME

CHAPTER ONE - SARAH

June 13, 2006

I have no idea what made him open up to me that day.

I pushed open the creaky screen door, calling, "Hey, Grandaddy, it's me!" even though I knew he wouldn't hear me. I tossed my keys on the small table by the front door, frowning slightly as they landed next to a mason jar containing a haphazard collection of plastic daisies and fabric carnations. My Granny Patsy would have pitched a fit. Every spring and summer, the old farmhouse was full of mason jars of fresh wildflowers and beautiful hydrangeas from the bushes she tended along the side of the house. She loved making colorful arrangements, but she couldn't stand artificial flowers.

When I reached the back door, I stood watching my grandfather for a few minutes. I noticed his drooping shoulders and his thinning white hair, which used to be jet black just like mine. I remembered the grandfather from my youth - one of the strongest, hardest working men I had ever met. A farmer by trade, he grew burley tobacco in the fields behind the house until arthritis and my mother's nagging finally wore him down enough to make him stop.

Now, the old tobacco barn looked as weathered and tired as he did, and the land was leased out to younger farmers who grew rows and rows of soybeans. Spring had been a wet one, so the planting happened later than normal. Although several weeks had passed, the tiny soybean plants were just starting to inch upward.

I wonder if he somehow sensed me standing there, looking out at the fields. He glanced over his shoulder and broke into a grin. "Well, lookee here who came to see me!" he said.

I smiled and stepped over to give him a gentle hug. He squeezed me back hard, proving that he may have appeared to be a tired old man, but he still held a quiet strength inside.

“How’ve you been, Grandaddy?” I said as I scooted the old cane-backed chair a little closer.

"Oh, fair to middlin', I'd say. How's them classes?"

"Ugh, don't remind me. I'm drowning in research papers and reading assignments. I don't know what I was thinking, going back to school after all these years. It was so much easier the first time around."

Grandaddy nodded his head solemnly while he listened, as if my classes and responsibilities were the most difficult things in the world to manage. I was painfully reminded that he had dropped out of school at the age of thirteen to help with the family farm. What did he know about graduate classes and research projects?

I took a deep breath and gave him a sheepish smile. "I'm sorry, Grandaddy. Here I am, dumping all of this on you before I even said a proper hello." I patted his wrinkled hand gently. "Mama said you've still been feeling sick the past couple of weeks. I'm sorry I didn't stop by sooner to check in on you. Is everything okay?"

"Aw, I'm fine, I'm fine." He shook his head. "I'm just gettin' old. Things seem to take a little longer for me to get over nowadays, that's all. Don't you worry your pretty little head about not stoppin' in for a visit here lately. I know you're workin' hard on them classes. Before long, I reckon you can quit workin' for that Mark feller and open up your own place. I can see the sign on the door now, Sarah Harper, Attorney at Law."

I laughed. "Well, I'm glad at least one of us thinks I'll make it to graduation."

He smiled and turned to stare at the tree line beyond the field. "Your Granny sure was proud of you, Baby Girl, and I am, too."

To my horror, I felt my eyes well up with tears. Why could I not visit him for five minutes without crying?

He turned back to me. "You want some sweet tea? I forgot to ask. Got a fresh pitcher in there. There's fresh mint leaves in the green bowl by the stove, too."

"Aw, no thanks, Grandaddy, I'm good. I just stopped by to check on you, but I can't stay long. I need to to go to the library so I can research for this paper I have to write. I'm such a slow writer, I need to get started on it right away. I also promised Steve I'd be back in time for dinner since he's been gone all week."

As soon as the words left my mouth, the familiar guilt crept back in. Why did I have to make visiting him sound like a burden, like everything else in my life was so important that stopping by to visit was an inconvenience intruding in my already too busy world?

"That's fine, darlin.' You're a busy gal with a lot goin' on. I been worryin' 'bout you, too. You feelin' okay? You look tired. Doctors say everything's all right now?"

He looked out at the fields, and I was thankful he couldn't see the tears in my eyes.

I nodded before answering quietly, "Yes, Grandaddy, I'm okay."

"And Steve? He's handlin' everything okay?"

"Yes, he's fine. We're both fine."

"Well, I'm sure your time will come, Baby Girl. You and Steve will make mighty fine parents one day. You just gotta wait for the good Lord's timin'. It'll happen when it's supposed to."

I swallowed and nodded, not trusting my voice.

"You know, I sure am glad you came by to visit. I told your mama I hadn't seen you in awhile and was hopin' you'd come check on your ol' Grandaddy sometime soon," he grinned.

"I know. I'm sorry," I said, thankful for the change in subject. "I meant to stop by earlier, but it's been a struggle this week. I'll be so glad when Mark is done with this trial. I think I must have scheduled thirty interviews and depositions yesterday. I'm so tired after work, I barely have the energy to throw something together for dinner or straighten the house, let alone work on my stuff for school. Steve's home now, thank goodness, so I have a little extra help, but I still haven't even started on this dang paper for my Legal Ethics class."

"Sounds like you sure got some plates spinnin," he said as he took a sip of his sweet tea.

"That's for sure. This research paper is gonna be the death of me. We're supposed to write a paper about an ethical issue related to criminal justice that set a precedent, like something that changed a law or the judicial system. I have no idea where to even start." I sighed with frustration, remembering the hours I had already spent researching at the library, only to find myself back at square one.

"Somethin' that changed the system. Well, pickin' a topic like that ought to be easy enough, I would think."

"Well, yeah. I mean, there are tons of examples throughout history of cases that changed the system. Brown versus Board of Education. Roe versus Wade. But there are so many cases, it's overwhelming. I keep picking an idea and then scrapping it." I felt my words speeding up and my anxiety level rising as they gained momentum. "This professor is impossible, too. He expects us to submit a topic proposal and detailed outline by the end of this week. This paper is a huge part of our semester grade, and you know how writing has always been so hard for me." I rubbed angrily at my eyes, hoping to wipe away the tears of frustration before they could spill over. "There's no way I'm going to pass this class."

Grandaddy didn't say anything for a moment, and I wondered if he was gearing up to give me a motivational speech about how hard work pays off, or how nothing easy is worth having, or how I needed to "keep chuggin' along" and things would work out all right in the end. I was again reminded that my grad school and office work frustrations were probably a foreign concept to him. Now the weather, the price of tobacco - those were things worth worrying about.

When he finally spoke, his words surprised me. "Well, now, maybe you should write about Daniel Porter."

"Who?"

"Daniel Porter." He paused long enough to take a sip of his sweet tea. "He was a colored boy that was hanged in Waverly back in '36."

"Really? I don't guess I've ever heard of him."

"Well, it was the last public hangin' that happened in the U.S." he said.

"Wow. And it happened right here in Waverly?" I asked, my eyes widening.

"Sure did." He nodded and took another long sip of his tea before continuing. "Yep. They built a great big ol' gallows downtown. I don't remember for sure, but seems like it was close to where the courthouse is now. The sheriff in charge at the time was a woman. People came to Waverly from all over to see a hangin' with a woman in charge."

I racked my brain for any long forgotten article or story I had read about Daniel Porter.

He went on, "The papers had story after story 'bout the crowds of people gatherin' to watch. Made Waverly look like a town full of bloodthirsty savages. All that bad publicity meant no judge in their right mind wanted to do a public hangin' after that. I reckon you could say it changed the system, all right."

"And when did you say this happened?" I asked.

"Back in '36, before your Granny Patsy and I got married. I left Louisville and moved back to Waverly that spring, matter of fact."

"So let me get this straight. A woman was the sheriff in Waverly back in 1936? And she was in charge of overseeing what turned out to be the last public execution in America?"

"Yep, that's right."

"And you remember hearing about this, like when it actually happened?"

"Why, 'course I remember it, Baby Girl." He slowly turned to look at me. "I was there."

CHAPTER TWO – LILLIAN

April 13, 1936

The coffin rested on the kitchen table in the center of the room.

She turned and stared at the walls, up at the ceiling, down at the floor, anything to avoid looking at the smooth pine box that seemed to swallow the air in this room, seemed to draw the very breath from her lungs.

She had always loved this room.

She remembered being a young newlywed in this house, hanging the pretty new curtains she'd made, Everett watching proudly from the doorway.

Four years later, this was the room where Everett could barely contain his excitement when she told him that finally, *finally*, the Lord had answered their prayers and seen fit to bless them with the baby they longed for. And then He blessed them with three more in His own good time, each one a miracle in Lillian's eyes.

This was the room where Mary, their eldest, had shown off her new dress before her first school dance. She had twirled around in a circle until she was dizzy and stumbling, and her younger brothers had howled with laughter.

They sang "Happy Birthday" only a few weeks ago in this room. She remembered Everett laughing and smearing a dab of frosting onto Patrick's nose.

But now this room would forever hold different memories for her.

Looking at the door would remind her of the long line of friends and neighbors who came through this morning to pay their respects.

The side table by the kitchen doorway, normally a gathering place for a vase of flowers and a stack of newspapers, was covered with an overflow of casseroles and fruit cobblers brought by the ladies from church.

And, of course, she would always remember the long, smooth sides of the large pine box resting on the table in the center of the room. The box that was the source of her anguish, the symbol of her torment, the reason she couldn't breathe.

It had been a long, dreadful day, and her shoulders ached. The clock on the wall sounded unbelievably loud. Or maybe the rhythmic pounding she heard was only in her head. She couldn't be sure.

She wanted nothing more than to take her hair down from the tight bun at the base of her neck, crawl into bed, and pretend that none of this had happened. That Everett was at work and would be home later for dinner, like always. She placed her hands over her face to block out the light. Her eyes felt scratchy, as though they were full of sand.

Mrs. Suzanne Bower suddenly appeared in front of her with a cup of hot tea. "Here, dear, drink this."

Mrs. Bower was the first to arrive that morning, as was her custom when there was a death in Waverly. As head of the local Baptist Women's Missionary Union, she took it upon herself to organize meals and help out with whatever the family of the deceased needed, whether it be funeral arrangements, childcare, meals, or a shoulder to cry on. She had been fulfilling this solemn duty for as long as most people in Waverly could remember, ever since her own husband died unexpectedly many years ago.

"Thank you," Lillian whispered.

"You're welcome, my dear," Mrs. Bower said, sitting delicately on the couch beside her. "You know, pneumonia is what took my Robert, too. Hard to believe he's been gone thirty years now."

Lillian glanced at her and sipped the tea, the hot liquid soothing her raw throat, though it did nothing for the ache in her chest. She tried to imagine thirty years without Everett, but found it to be an impossible task.

"Lillian, I want you to know something." The elderly woman reached a warm, wrinkled hand over and gripped Lillian's fingers tightly. "Life is hard, and it often doesn't turn out the way we expect. I can't tell you that it will get easier, that the pain will go away, but I can tell you that you will survive this. Even though it may feel right now like you can't go on another minute, you are capable of more than you know."

Lillian smiled weakly. "I appreciate that."

"If you ever need to talk, dear, I would certainly welcome your company any time."

Lillian exhaled a long, ragged breath. She wished she could tell this thoughtful woman how much she truly appreciated her kindness, thank her for bringing over breakfast that morning, for staying to oversee the visitors and rows of covered dishes parading through the house all afternoon. Lillian wanted to ask her how she was supposed to survive this, to tell her that she didn't feel strong at all, in fact she felt not just weak, but cracked and broken, like a part of her was damaged beyond repair. She wanted to tell her she was angry, so angry at the unfairness of it all. Angry at Everett, angry at God, angry at the church ladies who stopped by to drop off casseroles and pies before going home to their families and their strong, healthy husbands. But she simply didn't have the energy or the words to describe her anger or her pain. And yet, when she looked into Mrs. Bower's kind blue eyes, an understanding passed between them, and Lillian knew she didn't need to say a word.

Mrs. Bower returned to the kitchen, leaving Lillian to sip her tea and avoid looking at the pine box. Murmuring voices drifted in from the kitchen, but she could only make out occasional snatches of her neighbors' whispered conversations. "*... judge will need to decide ... too soon ... the children ...*"

The children.

They sat stiffly in the wooden kitchen chairs that had been moved into the sitting room, lost in their own thoughts, their eyes glazed over. The older boys, sixteen-year old Jack and Patrick, who had recently turned ten, stared down at the floor, their dark hair falling into their eyes. They were both in need of a haircut, but Lillian had no idea when she would be able to pick up a pair of scissors and do something as mundane as cutting hair. The effort of just breathing and holding back the tide of sorrow inside seemed to take all of her energy now.

Her youngest, eight year-old James, occasionally wiped his big brown eyes with the back of his hand. She knew he hated to cry in front of his brothers. Still, she saw the tears glistening on his thick, dark lashes that were so much like Everett's.

In the chair closest to the kitchen sat her beautiful eighteen year-old daughter, Mary, her red rimmed eyes staring hollowly at a lace handkerchief in her lap. Mary's long, dark hair, her pride and joy, had loosened from its ribbon and now cascaded around her shoulders, but she didn't seem to notice.

Lillian sighed.

One more day. Just one more day of this, and then the pine box would be taken away. it would be over, and she could go on with her life. Or what was left of it.

She tried to imagine fixing breakfast each morning for five instead of six.

"Mrs. Conner?"

She realized a familiar man was sitting on the couch next to her. Had he been there the whole time? She couldn't be sure.

"We all thought so much of your husband, Mrs. Conner," he said.

"Thank you," she said. She searched his face, taking in the cleft chin, the remarkably bright blue eyes. His name suddenly came to her. Judge Riney. Of course.

"Everett was a fine man, and you and your children have my deepest sympathy."

She smiled. "I appreciate your kind words, Judge Riney. My Everett is ... was ... indeed one of a kind."

The judge nodded, looking at the pine box. Lillian wondered if it made him as uncomfortable as it did her.

"Mrs. Conner," he turned to her, "This may seem terribly insensitive, but there's something I need to ask. I'm afraid your husband's untimely passing has left us in an awkward position, without a sheriff in Clay County."

She nodded absently.

He looked at her children, who were all watching and listening intently. "And the truth is ... well, I may be able to offer a rather unorthodox solution that will be mutually beneficial."

She sipped her tea and waited, wishing he would make his point.

"If you would be willing to consider it," Judge Riney said, "there is a statute in place that could help us with filling the role of sheriff and also provide you with an income, at least temporarily." He paused before continuing. "What I'm trying to say is, would you be willing to step in as sheriff in your husband's place?"

She sat staring at him, dumbfounded.

"It would only be until a proper election this fall, of course," he added.

"I don't understand," she said as her foggy mind struggled to make sense of his words. "You want me to take Everett's place? As sheriff of Clay County?"

"Yes, ma'am. The statute allows for the county judge to appoint a successor if the sheriff's position becomes ... well, if it becomes open due to unforeseen circumstances. In addition, deputies cannot serve without a sheriff in place, so we've found ourselves in a tight spot. I'm sure you understand we need to find a replacement as soon as possible. In light of your current situation, and in honor of your husband, whom we all held in such high regard, I would like to formally offer you this position. That is, if you're willing to accept."

Lillian turned slowly and looked at the four young faces staring at her, wide-eyed. She swallowed and turned back to Judge Riney. "Judge, I thank you for your consideration, truly. And I am honored that you would place your confidence and trust in me. But what would people think if I was sworn in as sheriff? I have no experience, no credentials to make me qualified for such a role. I'm nothing but a mother and a simple housewife. Surely you have someone else more qualified in mind, maybe a deputy or an officer with at least some kind of experience?"

"Please consider it, Mrs. Conner. This would provide an income to help you care for the children, at least until you can get on your feet. Seeing the doubt on her face, he continued, "This will allow us to help you and honor your husband's memory. I've spoken with the other officers, and they are one hundred percent in support of this arrangement. Deputy Mitchell has assured me he will personally guide you every step of the way."

She remembered how much Everett respected Deputy Mitchell, how the kindhearted young deputy even joined them for dinner on occasion, devouring her peach cobbler as though he had never eaten in his life.

She looked again at her children's faces. Her children that were now depending on her to be both mother and father, to provide for them. Her children that would need her now more than ever.

She turned back to Judge Riney's hopeful face. She knew very well that she was not cut out to be a sheriff. She hadn't the first clue about running a police station. But it seemed Everett had found a way to provide for them, to take care of them all, even after he was gone.

For the first time since before she heard her husband exhale his last, ragged breath, Lillian felt a tiny flame of hope. Maybe, just maybe it could work.

CHAPTER THREE - SALLY

June 6, 1936

Sally put the last of the beer glasses away, wiped down the counter, turned out the light above the bar, and tried not to think about how tired she was. Saturday nights at the tavern were always busy, but her latest fight with Daniel had left her drained in a way no amount of physical exertion ever could. It seemed their arguments lately were like taking out the trash or washing the dishes - unpleasant, but unavoidable.

It wasn't always that way, of course. He knew how to flash that special grin when he wanted something, and she fell for it every single time. He could always make her laugh, even after a hard day at Tiegg's, her back aching from carrying trays all day. But when his temper flared, it was best to stand aside. She absently glanced down at the purplish bruises on her wrist, as if she needed proof.

She took off her apron and hung it on the nail by the kitchen door. She walked to the front table by the window and dropped into a chair, sighing heavily at the pile of bread crumbs on the floor. She had forgotten to sweep under this table when the last customer had finally stumbled out. Hershel probably wouldn't notice, but Sally prided herself on keeping the tavern spotlessly clean.

She rubbed her fingers absently across the wood grain of the table and thought back to the night she had first met Daniel Porter in this very room.

He had strolled in and pulled up a stool at the bar, flashing her a smile almost as soon as he sat down. She knew most of the folks in Waverly, but she couldn't remember seeing him before that night. He was a small man, almost delicate, and his dark eyes seemed to bore right into her. She was sure she'd remember if she had met him before.

They had been busy that night, but she remembered refilling his glass several times over the next hour while he entertained her with stories of growing up in Virginia and making his own way after losing both of his parents. He had lived with his sister and her family for a time, but his sister's husband made it clear that it was only a temporary arrangement. Daniel found himself in "a spot of trouble," as he put it, and decided it was time to leave Virginia.

Sally hadn't asked what kind of trouble, though she guessed from the way he threw back his whiskey that it may have involved his drinking habits. She knew all about that. She grew up watching her daddy in the evenings with a bottle of cheap whiskey on the table, a glass of the potent liquid in his shaky hand.

Daniel told her he had landed in Louisville first, working at a bourbon distillery, sweeping floors, packing crates, and slipping a bottle or two in his pockets now and then. He soon grew restless and decided to try Waverly. He'd heard there were plenty of jobs in the growing town situated on the banks of the Ohio River, so he hitched a ride on a truck from the distillery. Since his arrival in Waverly, he had worked for the Andersons and done some odd jobs for Delbert Moore, who allowed him to rent a room.

Sally remembered wiping down the bar at the tavern that night, listening to Daniel tell his story, until he stopped suddenly. Taking a last swig of his drink, he put down the empty glass and said, "Well, I reckon that's enough about me. What's your story, doll?"

She had grinned shyly back at him, shrugged, and smoothed back the strands of frizzy hair that had escaped her bun. She told him she was from a small town, her mama died young, and her daddy worked in the fields when he wasn't trying to drown his pain in a bottle of whiskey.

Daniel nodded as he listened to her talk, and she sensed he understood her longing to escape, to see what else might be out there. So she told him how she waited until her daddy was drunk one night, the empty whiskey bottle standing at attention on the table in front of him. She slipped into his room, took the cash from the coffee can on the top shelf of his closet, hitched a ride to Waverly, and never looked back.

She was fourteen years old the day she arrived in Waverly.

She had wandered around town for an hour before noticing Hershel Tiegg sweeping the front stoop below the Tiegg's Tavern sign. She took a deep breath and walked right up to him, introduced herself as seventeen year old Sally Davidson, and asked for a job. Hershel was impressed by her seemingly confident manner, and truth be told, he was desperate after losing his best server the week before. He gave her a job washing dishes, and she'd been there ever since, saving money until she could go to Louisville and get a nice place of her own.

Daniel had smiled and shook his head at her.

"What?" she asked, suddenly defensive.

"Oh, nothin'. Just not many girls with that kind of gumption 'round here," he said, and she realized with relief that his smile was one of admiration and not mocking. He wasn't dismissing her dream of moving to Louisville as something impossible or silly.

Oh, how she had loved that about him.

She told him how she had heard all about the famous Brown Hotel from Hershel, who had grown up in Louisville. He had told her about the glittering chandeliers, the wealthy guests who came from all over. She longed to see such a dazzling place in person, hoped to work there one day, maybe cleaning or cooking in the restaurant.

"Wait, you mean you ain't seen it?" Daniel asked, surprised. "Aw, Miss Sally, it sure is somethin' else. I walked by there all the time back when I lived in Louisville. There's fancy cars that come rollin' right up to the front. They have a man standing outside all day just to open the door. Can you imagine? A man who gets paid to open the hotel door for people to come on in! Now, that's a job even I could do!" He threw back his head and laughed heartily, his white teeth gleaming in the lamplight, and she laughed with him, marveling at this handsome man who had taken such an interest in her. "Who knows, Miss Sally? Maybe I'll take you there one day," he said with a wink.

But that was months ago. Before she met the other Daniel. The Daniel with flashing, angry eyes and whiskey on his breath. The one who could raise his fists with dizzying speed, striking her body while somehow simultaneously managing to pound at her very soul. How was he able to make her feel shattered on the inside and on the outside, all at the same time?

Still, Daniel loved her. She knew he did.

He was a paradox - a man made of two halves, two distinct personalities trapped in the same wiry body. He was hard, yet loving, complex, yet simple. He would bring her a beautiful bouquet of hand-picked wildflowers one day, then smash the vase against the wall in a drunken rage the next. With tears streaming down his face and heartfelt apologies tumbling out of his mouth, he would kiss the very bruises he had caused.

Life had been one long struggle for Daniel Porter since he had arrived in Waverly, and oh, how Sally's heart was broken, not merely *by* him, but *for* him, time after time. Her heart broke for the man he was, but also for the man she knew he could be, if only given the chance.

She remembered when he came to her back in February, shamefaced that he had been fired from another job, asking to borrow a little money for the rent, promising to pay her back. She couldn't stand to see the look of despair in his eyes, so she gave the money willingly, knowing that it would delay their plans to make it to Louisville.

Their plans. He had become a part of her dream now, a part of her future at the Brown Hotel. And come hell or high water, she knew they'd get there one day.

CHAPTER FOUR – DANIEL

June 7, 1936

Rivulets of sweat slowly trickled down his back, and his thin cotton shirt was clinging to his skin. The temperature was already rising, humidity thickening the air. An oppressive heat wave had been suffocating Waverly for nearly two weeks, and it didn't seem to be leaving anytime soon.

Wide-eyed, he leaned out over the window sill and peered left, right, and then left again before climbing out. He crouched low and tried to slow his breathing. Every step he took set the worn wooden planks to groaning, the sound amplified in the silent, early morning darkness. He moved to the end of the walkway, then stepped over the rail and across the small gap to the roof of the adjacent garage, back the way he came, before dropping carefully down to the ground below. When he landed, a sharp stab of pain in his foot caused him to stumble a bit. He limped into the shadows against the building, shifted the wadded up fabric bundle under his arm, willed his hammering heart to slow, and patted his pockets. The rings were still there.

The Smiths would be up early. Mrs. Smith's habit of cooking a full, early Sunday morning breakfast was well-known to everyone on the block. Many a Sunday morning, he had laid awake on his cot in the cabin behind Delbert Moore's place and smelled the pleasing aroma of bacon, eggs, and fried potatoes drifting in through the open window. He tried to time it so he would casually stroll by right as they were finishing breakfast, and sure enough, it had paid off more than once. Mrs. Smith would open the door, call him over, and give him a tin pan filled with biscuits and sausage gravy, or fried eggs and bacon. Once, she even offered him a whole plate of cornbread and fried ham. The Smiths had always been good neighbors to him.

Sighing with relief at having made it this far, he stepped through his cabin door, put the fabric bundle on the side table, and grabbed a stained handkerchief. He wiped the sweat from his face, forehead, and neck. He stared down at his hands, which were still throbbing. He turned them over and studied them for any scratches or marks, anything suspicious. He flexed his fingers slowly, squeezing them into a fist and then releasing them. The sorc muscles in his forearms and hands screamed in protest, so he shook his arms out gently and rolled his shoulders and neck.

After another deep breath, he took the rings out of his pocket and held them in his palm. They felt surprising heavy, for such small objects.

He recalled the first time he saw those rings sitting on her bureau, just right out there in the open. It had been an unseasonably warm day in early May. He had crawled out of bed at first light, despite a hangover, figuring he would have a better chance at finding some work if he got started early.

He remembered standing on the porch that morning in May and squinting against the bright sunlight, his head pounding as he considered his limited options. Nathaniel King hired a couple of boys earlier that week to help clear his lower field. He didn't know if Mr. King would still need help, but it might be worth hitching a ride out to his farm to check.

He was lost in his thoughts when he heard the old lady call down to him from her second floor window. "Daniel? Would you be a dear and come help me? I want to move a bureau to the south wall of this room, but it's dreadfully heavy, and I can't seem to get it to budge."

He called back, "Yes, Mrs. Bower, ma'am. I'll come right now," and hurried over to her door. He was behind on rent again, so he hoped Mrs. Bower would be feeling generous.

When he stepped inside, he nearly knocked over a bucket sitting near the doorway. "Watch your step, now," she said sharply. "I've been moppin' floors all morning."

He nodded and carefully followed her up the narrow staircase, down the hall to the back bedroom.

"Now, this here is what I'm wanting to move. See that empty space over there on that wall? I'd like to slide this bureau over there, but I can't seem to move it. Maybe you'll have better luck than me."

Daniel nodded and replied, "Well, ma'am, I'll sure give it a try." He gripped the heavy piece of furniture on either side and dragged it across the floor, grunting and straining with effort. His short stature and slight frame did not make heavy lifting easy, but he was stronger than he looked.

When he was finished, Mrs. Bower clapped with delight. "Well, young man, you sure made that look easy!" She handed him two quarters from her change purse, which was more than he expected.

As he bowed his head and mumbled a quick, "Thank you, ma'am," he glanced to the right and saw a small ivory dish sitting on her dressing table containing an array of rings and sparkling hat pins. Its contents glittered and shined in the morning sunlight streaming through the window. Next to the dish was a small box, opened to reveal a milky white strand of pearls and a shiny gold chain.

Daniel smiled at the memory from that day in May, at his shock the first time he glimpsed how much wealth Mrs. Suzanne Bower had accumulated over the years.

Using his thumb and index finger, he rubbed the gold band of the largest ring that he now held in his palm. He was in awe of how smooth it was. Unblemished. Jewelry like this was surely worth a fortune. He turned the ring over and peered closely at the large diamond.

He knew Sally had some crazy idea about going to Louisville, but he'd found nothing but trouble since coming to Kentucky. It was time to go back home to Virginia. And as he slipped the rings back in his pants pocket, he knew he had finally found a way to get there.

CHAPTER FIVE - SARAH

June 13, 2006

I sat in stunned silence. *He had been there?*

Grandaddy looked down, lost in his thoughts, folding and unfolding his calloused hands in his lap. I waited, the only sound coming from the bees buzzing among the flowers.

"Your Granny's hydrangeas sure look pretty today, don't they?" he asked with a nod in their direction. "She sure did love them flowers."

I followed his gaze, marveling at his obvious attempt to change the subject. My sweet Granny had been gone almost a year, but her beautiful blue and white hydrangeas still bloomed all along the side of the house. It seemed they'd been there for as long as I could remember.

My mother and I first moved into the old farmhouse with Grandaddy James and Granny Patsy when I was four.

An icy highway had taken my father away from us and left my fun-loving, affectionate mother drowning in a river of painful grief. I became an orphan, though one parent still lived - barely.

Our stay of a few months turned into a few years. It took that long for my mother to scratch and claw her way out of the deep, dark hole she had fallen into.

My summer days were spent on the tractor with Grandaddy, surrounded by the smell of his Old Spice aftershave and the sound of buzzing insects. He taught me how to tell when the never-ending rows of burley tobacco plants were ready for topping, their pink and white blooms just beginning to show.

I remember working with Granny Patsy in the kitchen while my mother took her afternoon nap, which lasted most of the day. I would balance on a kitchen chair, giggling at my flour-covered hands as Granny showed me how to roll the dough and cut out circles for biscuits with an upside down mason jar. Once the biscuits were in the oven and everything was washed and dried, we'd go out back to pick fresh hydrangeas to put in the mason jar and set it in the center of the worn, oak table.

Grandaddy glanced over at me and cleared his throat, bringing me rushing back to the present. "Yep, your granny sure did love her flowers."

"Yeah, she did," I nodded impatiently. "But Grandaddy, I don't understand. You were actually there the day of that execution?"

He sighed. "Yep, I was, but people 'round here mostly want to forget about that summer, hon."

"Why?"

"Well, it made the town look bad, that's all." He frowned. "The murder was bad enough, but then the crowds showin' up and them damned reporters spreadin' their lies just made it ten times worse. Everybody just wanted to pretend it didn't happen."

"Wait, you said the reporters spread lies. What kinds of lies?" I asked.

"Oh, they made Waverly look like a bunch of savages," his voice grew hard and he shook his head. "Made it sound like we threw a carnival party at the gallows. There sure wasn't no partyin' that day, I can tell you that much. And poor Sheriff Conner did her best to keep things under control, but them reporters kept stirrin' things up."

"Who was she? The sheriff, I mean?"

"Lillian Conner. Her husband, I believe Everett was his name, had been the sheriff. She took over the job when he passed," he said.

None of this was making sense, and I wondered suddenly if Grandaddy was somehow getting the details mixed up in his mind.

"Yep, I reckon she did the best she could, given the circumstances," he continued.

"So she became the new sheriff just because her husband died? Wasn't there someone else who could've taken over instead? Like maybe a deputy or something? I mean, when I think of law enforcement in 1936, a female sheriff is definitely not the first thing that comes to mind. Especially in Waverly. We're not exactly known as a hotbed for progressive feminism, you know."

Grandaddy chuckled softly. "Well, when her husband passed, she was left with four young'uns to tend to, and the law said it was up to the county judge to appoint somebody to take over 'til the next election. The Conner family sure was looked up to in them days. Her husband dyin' like that sure was a shock, and I reckon folks in Waverly felt kindly sorry for her. If she was sheriff, she'd at least have a way to provide for her young'uns."

I thought about this amazing woman who had experienced such tremendous loss, and yet somehow found the strength to raise four children on her own while serving as the county sheriff. Not only that, but she did it in an era when most women didn't work outside the home.

"So what about the guy who was hanged? Who'd he kill?" I said.

Grandaddy suddenly seemed uncomfortable. "Well, they didn't exactly hang him for killin' somebody."

"Wait, if he didn't kill anybody, what did he do?" I tried to think of other possible crimes heinous enough to result in public execution. Maybe he was an arsonist who terrorized the town. Maybe he had gone on a rampage in a saloon. Did they even have mass shootings in 1936? Or maybe Grandaddy was mixing up the details. I studied his lined face for any sign of confusion, any sign that his memories were cloudy. How could he have mentioned a murder, and then moments later claim Daniel Porter wasn't hanged for killing someone?

Grandaddy sighed and looked down at his wrinkled hands resting on his knees. "Baby Girl, some things are just better left in the past."

"Yeah, I get that, Grandaddy, but I'm just trying to understand what happened."

"You're about as stubborn as a mule, you know that?" he said, exasperated.

"So I've been told. It's a trait I inherited from my grandfather." I winked at him.

He chuckled. "Well, you got me there, I reckon. If you must know, they hanged that boy for takin' advantage of an ol' widow lady. Everybody knew he killed her, though."

I searched his face, more confused than ever. "Wait, if she was killed in the attack, why didn't they charge him with murder?"

Grandaddy looked uncomfortable. "I told you, it was complicated."

"Complicated how?"

"Oh, I can't remember everything, Sarah. It was a long time ago. But I do know that boy was guilty, and that's a fact."

"How can you be so sure?"

"Well, for one thing, he confessed, and I don't recollect he had much of a defense, so to speak. There weren't no witnesses to testify, so the whole thing was over right quick. The jury only took a few minutes to decide he should be hanged," he said.

"Wait, no defense? And the jury returned with a death sentence in a matter of minutes? How did that happen?"

I noticed a fierceness in his watery blue eyes. "Look, he was a colored boy who attacked and killed a white woman in 1936. Things in Waverly was just different back then." He sipped his tea. "Just forget I mentioned it, Baby Girl. I'm sorry I even brought it up. Best just to leave it in the past. I'm sure you'll think of somethin' else for that paper you need to write."

I nodded absently as I thought of the Waverly I knew, where folks traded recipes and fishing stories and neighbors looked out for one another, a town of big Sunday dinners and 4th of July parades through the downtown streets.

But what if this town of warm smiles and friendly waves was something else? What if there was a layer of something ugly and rotting hiding behind the mask of kindly neighbors and church potlucks?

What if the Waverly I knew wasn't really Waverly at all?

CHAPTER SIX - DANIEL

June 7, 1936

He couldn't remember what on earth had made him think going to see Mr. Anderson last December was a good idea.

He had stumbled out of the tavern and strolled down to the river to watch the moonlight reflecting like diamonds on the water. He leaned against the railing and wished he could hitch a ride down the Ohio River to a new town. A new life.

Sometime later, he walked down First Street, deserted and quiet in the frigid night air, and saw the Andersons' cabin. Mr. Anderson hired him once before to help replace some floorboards on the back porch. He was a hard man to work for, prone to angry outbursts, but

Daniel was desperate. Work in Waverly had been hard to come by anyway, but now it was damn near impossible to find a decent wage. How could he earn enough money to go back home if he was constantly losing out on jobs and being harassed by the police?

No one answered the door when he knocked, so he reached a hand out and turned the cold metal knob, not expecting it to move. When the door swung open, he stumbled forward and nearly fell into the darkened front room before regaining his balance.

Embers glowed in the fireplace, and he smelled the delicious cinnamon aroma of Mrs. Anderson's famous apple pie, which sat on the sideboard table under a dish towel.

"Boy, what in the hell are you doing here?" Mr. Anderson's angry whisper caught him off guard.

"Evenin', Mr. Anderson," Daniel bowed his head. His words sounded slurred, even to his own ears. "Sure am sorry to bother you, sir, but I'm in a tight spot and need to find me some work. I thought you might be needin' some more help 'round here, and seein' as I helped you awhile back with them floorboards, I figured maybe…"

"Are you drunk?" Anderson hissed.

Daniel shook his head a little too quickly, causing the room to spin around him. "No sir, no..."

"Have you lost your damn mind?" Anderson said, growing louder. "Do you even know what time it is?"

"I know it's late, sir, and I'm sorry, but I'd be much obliged if you'd just let me explain…"

"No, boy, you let me explain," Anderson snapped, jabbing his calloused finger towards Daniel's face. "You've got no business on my property in the middle of the night, let alone bargin' into my house uninvited. You people need to remember your place 'round here."

Daniel's blood boiled.

"Did you hear me, boy? I know you ain't got a lick o' brains in that head of yours, but are you deaf, too?" Mr. Anderson asked, his pudgy face red with rage. He took another step towards Daniel. "I said get outta my house before I call the law!"

Daniel stood his ground a moment longer, breathing hard and flexing his fists, before finally turning back towards the door. Mr. Anderson practically shoved him out, still threatening to call the law.

And call the law he did. But Daniel knew he hadn't actually done anything wrong. Why else would the charges have been dropped to "drunk and disorderly" instead of burglary? It was a misunderstanding, that's all.

Still, he sure was getting sick and tired of folks like Mr. Anderson.

And now this. Just a few months later, and he was in trouble again. Big trouble this time.

It wasn't supposed to happen like this. He had a plan, and he had been so very careful. But they would be after him again. It was just a matter of time. Since the Anderson incident, whenever there was trouble, they always came looking for him. If Mr. Koll reported some missing items from his store, the police were sure to come to Daniel's door, poking around and asking questions. Someone threw a rock and broke a window at the A&P late one night, and the police showed up at Daniel's door within the hour. Another time, he got into an argument with the bartender at Tiegg's, and the next thing you know, he was in a jail cell with a deputy telling him he needed to "sleep it off."

He was lucky to have made it this far, but his luck wasn't going to last much longer. The police were sure to come snooping around his cabin soon, and he had to make sure they didn't find anything.

Despite a slight limp from his aching foot, he quickly crossed the narrow alley and then edged along the wall of Frank Newell's barn until he reached the door. Frank never used this barn anymore. He had paid Daniel months earlier to help cut boards for a newer storage building down the block. Once it was finished, this barn became nothing more than a graveyard for his abandoned projects and rusted out equipment.

Glancing both ways, Daniel wiped the sweat from his forehead, then gently slid the door's latch. He slipped inside and closed the heavy wooden door behind him. Beams of sunlight shining through the cracks in the old wood cut through the darkness of the barn's interior, and dust motes danced in the light. The smell of engine oil from the wrecked 1920 Model T that Frank couldn't bring himself to part with filled his nostrils. Rusted tools and equipment lined one entire wall, and several tables and sawhorses were littered with Frank's mostly unfinished projects. Dusty mason jars holding hinges, bolts, and nails of various sizes rested on a high shelf against the back wall. An old metal plate on the table closest to the door was home to a huge, hopelessly tangled ball of twine, and a jumble of tobacco sticks stood at attention against the far wall.

He shifted the fabric bundle to his other arm and then pulled the rings and necklace from his pants pocket. He stood a moment, feeling the weight of the jewels in his hand and the cool, liquid silk surface of the pearls. He tilted his hand a little to the left in a beam of sunlight and marveled at the sparkling trinkets he held.

He pocketed the jewels and put the fabric bundle in a box against the wall, covering it with an old horse blanket. With a backward glance, he bent to shift an old wooden trunk closer to the wall. He tested it with one foot and then, satisfied it would hold his weight, climbed gingerly on top. A taller man would've had no trouble reaching the shelf, but with a height of just five feet two inches, Daniel had always been a climber. It seemed things had been that way his entire life. He was always striving for something just out of reach.

He put the jewels on the shelf and reached for an old, slightly rusted can near the back. It was surprisingly light. He peered inside and saw some links from an old chain. Perfect.

He picked up the strand of pearls and held them close, marveling again at their smoothness. He touched them to his mouth and moved them slowly across his lips, not really knowing why.

In one fluid motion, he dropped the pearls inside, then grabbed the rings and dropped them in. He shook the can gently, watching the rings toss about on the bed of milky white pearls with a gentle *chink, chink, chink* sound. The sound of freedom.

He put the can back in its spot, pushing it all the way to the back of the shelf. He moved some other jars and cans in front of it and stepped down from the wooden trunk. He peered up, making sure nothing looked out of place. Satisfied, he dusted his hands off on his trouser legs and made his way back to the door.

He glanced around as he walked back across the alley, but no one was out and about. He wiped his brow and sighed with relief. Now he just needed to hide out until things cooled down, maybe over at Sally's place. The police wanted to blame him for everything? Well, they could go right ahead. Things had definitely not gone according to his plan that night, but they could search his room from top to bottom and never find a lick of evidence there to tie him to the crime.

And even if they did find some other way to come after him, he would just tell them the truth. Allen McDaniel had been in the old lady's room with him that night. And it was Allen McDaniel who killed her.

CHAPTER SEVEN - SARAH

June 15, 2006

"Are you okay?" Mark asked with concern.

I opened my eyes and glanced up sheepishly to see him standing in the office doorway, a stack of files in one hand and his lucky coffee mug in the other. I wondered how long he had been standing there watching me pinch the bridge of my nose, silently willing my tension headache to disappear.

"Yeah, I'm fine," I sighed. "Just finishing up this memo and then I can get to transcribing those last depositions. Sorry I'm putting you so far behind."

"Hey, no worries. It's been a busy week. Listen, I've been worried about you a lot the past few months, with everything you've been going through. I'm still not sure you took enough time off after ... you know, after..."

"I appreciate your concern, Mark," I interrupted, "but I'm fine. Really." I pasted a smile on my face, wondering if this was my life now - people always asking me how I feel, worrying about my health (and my sanity), me trying to convince them I was fine. Even if sometimes I wasn't.

"Well, I hope you know how much I appreciate all your hard work on this trial. You know I couldn't be this awesome without you, right?" he said, grinning.

I laughed. "Yes, sir, I am well aware of the direct correlation between my work ethic and your level of awesomeness."

"Of course you are! Hey, listen, I have a 1:30 at the courthouse and I'm sure it'll be a doozy, so I may not be back after lunch today. Leave those forms on my desk and I'll sign them in the morning."

"Sure thing!" I forced another cheerful smile as he turned and left, silently berating myself for forgetting about the stupid forms.

I spent the next two hours slogging through the forms and depositions for Mark's upcoming trial. Thankfully, the office phone was mostly silent, and I was able to finish what I needed to before heading out to lunch.

I drove quickly to the Clay County Library, where I had decided to spend my lunch break digging up whatever information I could find about Daniel Porter.

"Can I help you with something?"

I tried not to stare at the boy behind the desk. The name tag displayed on his blue polo shirt proved he was indeed an assistant librarian at the Clay County Library, but I still found myself scrutinizing the acne scattered across his forehead. He was a librarian? He barely looked old enough to drive.

"Um, yes, I hope so. I'm working on a research project for my grad class. I'm looking for some old newspaper articles and was wondering if you could point me in the right direction?"

"Sure, I'd be glad to," he said as he stood and gestured for me to follow him to the stairs. "All our newspaper files are kept in the Kentucky Room, which is downstairs. Some of them are in digital form now, but the really old ones are still on microfiche. We're working on transferring everything over. What year are you looking for?"

"I'm actually looking for information about something that happened in Waverly in 1936," I answered as we started down the stairs into the basement section of the library.

"Ah, you wouldn't happen to be researching the Daniel Porter case, would you?" he asked.

Shock registered on my face. "How did you know?"

He smiled as he held open the glass door to the Kentucky Room. "Well, now and then we get someone who comes in and asks about it. There's not a lot of other things of note that happened in Waverly 1936, at least not that people would bother to come research. If someone comes in asking for info about something that happened in Waverly in 1936, it usually has something to do with Daniel Porter."

"I see. Do a lot of people come here looking for info about him?"

"Not that many, but then again, I've only been here about a year. There are some old timers that come in and read the articles now and then, and a couple of months ago, a reporter from Louisville came. He was working on an article about important events in Kentucky's past, or something like that."

I followed him to a large filing cabinet. He removed a brown leather book from on top, placed it on a desk, and opened it. "Okay, so this logbook is our very old-fashioned method of keeping tabs on who accesses the files in this room. We've unfortunately had some thefts and vandalism in the past. Some of these artifacts are very old, so we can never be too careful."

I nodded and took in the rows of bookcases and filing cabinets, the large microfiche machines along the back wall.

"Most of the Porter files will be in reels in the third filing cabinet. The files and envelopes inside are labeled by month and year, so you just find the one you're looking for, take the microfiche reel out of the envelope, and put it in one of the machines."

He must have seen my doubtful expression because he smiled patiently and said, "Don't worry. Instructions are taped to the side of each machine."

"Okay, great," I said, relieved. "I don't think I've used one of those machines since I was in high school, and that was probably before you were born," I laughed. "Oh, no offense. I mean, it's just that you look kind of young for a librarian."

"I get that a lot," he said, rolling his eyes. "Anyway, we have a machine over in the corner back there if you want to print anything. It's 10-cents per page." He looked around. "Well, I think that about covers it. Don't forget to sign the logbook, and let me know if you have any questions."

"I sure will. Thanks so much for your help." I said as he left, the door closing behind him with a soft thud.

I glanced at the clock on the wall and realized with disappointment that I only had about twenty-five minutes of my lunch break left before I needed to get back to work. I dug through my handbag and found my change purse in the bottom. I began digging out coins to feed into the machine with one hand as I searched through the file drawer marked 1936 with the other. I grabbed some envelopes marked "August 1936 - Waverly Examiner" and rushed to the ancient machines along the back wall.

Minutes later, I found myself lost in the events of 1936. Even though Grandaddy said it was a huge news story, I was still amazed at the amount of press coverage the execution received. I sent page after page to the printer, stopping every few minutes to feed more coins into the machine. There were interviews with attorneys, printed letters from leaders in the black community, even photos of Porter and the infamous scaffold. But what surprised me the most were the photographs of the crowds at the execution.

I slowly turned the machine's knob and peered at the screen, studying a large grainy photograph of thousands of people gathered near the scaffold, which stood on a platform high above the onlookers. The caption described how the crowds had formed early that morning, everyone hoping to get a good view. A couple of ambitious young men sold sandwiches and drinks to spectators who were fearful they might lose their prime viewing spots if they left to go grab a bite to eat.

The bodies filled every available space, an endless sea of men in white shirts, some with hats, standing with arms crossed or hands on their hips. I wondered what thoughts were running through their heads as they watched, watching and waiting to see a man die. What must it have been like to watch him climb those thirteen steps to the gallows, to see the noose placed around his neck, to hear the spring of the trap when the lever was pulled?

I scrutinized the photo for a glimpse of Sheriff Lillian Conner. I counted no less than seven people standing on the scaffold's small platform with the prisoner, but she did not seem to be among them. In fact, it seemed that the crowd, especially those standing directly in front of the gallows, consisted entirely of men. Where was she? Did she stand next to the condemned man and pulled the lever, sending him to his death? Was she at the bottom of the steps, blending into the large crowd? Or had she been back at police headquarters, not wanting to witness the sentence her duty required her to carry out? No, she must have been there. Grandaddy said the entire country was focused on Waverly that summer to see a female sheriff preside over a public hanging. Surely she didn't skip out on the main event.

With a jolt, I suddenly remembered my grandfather's words - the words that started me on this mission to find out what happened in Waverly that summer. "Of course I remember it. I was there." I flipped through the pages, scanning the faces in each photograph, expecting at any moment to see Grandaddy's weathered face staring back out at me. But then I remembered he would have been in his early twenties at the time. I may not even have recognized him in 1936.

I glanced at the clock and realized my lunch break was almost over. With only minutes to spare, I threw the reels in the envelopes and crammed them back into the drawer. I grabbed my thick stack of pages from the machine and was turning to leave when I remembered the logbook. I rushed over to the desk and fumbled for a pen from the magnetic cup hanging on the side of the filing cabinet. I glanced absently at the list of names on the page as I touched pen to paper.

And then I dropped the pen in shock. There, in my grandfather's unmistakable scrawled handwriting next to yesterday's date, I saw his signature: "James Graham"

CHAPTER EIGHT - LILLIAN

June 7, 1936

"Ma'am, there's been … an incident."

Deputy Mitchell stood in the doorway, as if not quite sure whether he should enter the room or stay out in the hall. He cleared his throat and removed his hat, then smoothed a lock of blonde hair back from his pale forehead.

Lillian frowned at Mitchell's interruption as Father Stuart rose from his seat and moved towards the door. "Well, it sounds like you have some work to take care of, Sheriff. I'll be back to check on you again next week."

Lillian stood. "Thank you, Father. I can't tell you how much I appreciate your prayers."

The old priest smiled at her, then nodded to Deputy Mitchell before stepping out into the hall.

"Now, what kind of an incident, Mitchell?" Lillian said, clearly irritated. She sometimes got the impression that Mitchell, in particular, wasn't quite sure what to make of her new role. There had been talk among the other officers about Judge Riney's decision to appoint her, whether it was a wise decision or one sure to end in disaster. She knew the doubts and whispers comprised a battle she would face every single day. The men had highly respected her husband. But that didn't mean they were comfortable taking orders from his wife.

She began looking through the old wooden desk drawers. "Mitchell, do you know where Everett kept the extra pencils? I was working on updating some files, but this silly pencil I've been using is worn clean down to a nub."

"Ma'am," Mitchell said softly. "I'm afraid something terrible has happened."

Lillian stopped rifling through the doors and looked up at him. Her thoughts immediately flew to her children. She glanced at the clock and ticked off their whereabouts one by one. Mary would be working on her embroidery right about now and enjoying a little quiet time to herself before starting the dinner roast. Jack was supposed to be over at old Mr. Sawyer's helping him clean the barn while the younger boys went fishing with Mr. Sawyer's grandsons.

She looked back at Mitchell, too afraid to ask if her children were safe and unharmed. Instead, she waited.

"Well, ma'am ... it seems ... uh ..." Deputy Mitchell shifted his weight from one foot to the other. His eyes darted all around the room as if he wasn't sure where to look.

She took a deep breath and waited, not trusting her voice.

With a gulp, he glanced both ways down the hall before stepping into the office and closing the door. He finally looked her in the eye and said, "It looks like there's been a murder, ma'am."

She dropped heavily back into the chair as the air rushed out of her lungs. "A murder?" she whispered. "In Waverly?"

The young deputy nodded solemnly, and a thousand thoughts raced through her mind. Foremost among them was the same thought that haunted her on a daily basis in various forms: *why had Everett left her to bear this burden alone?* Oh, she certainly felt grateful for the work and the ability to earn an honest day's wage. Lord knows she needed an income, with four children to raise on her own.

And so far, everyone at the station had been accommodating, despite a few awkward exchanges and whispers. But she had been in office for less than two months. She still had so much to learn about the day to day operations of things. And now this? A murder?

"Who was it, Mitchell?" she asked, her voice cracking.

The story poured out of him. "Suzanne Bower. Mr. Smith, the downstairs neighbor, found her this morning. They fetched Doc Baker from the church, and he and the coroner went straight over. I just got off the phone with Mr. Smith. He's real tore up, as you can imagine."

Memories crashed over Lillian in waves. Mrs. Bower patting her hand and offering her condolences after Everett's funeral. (Had that been only a few months ago?) Sipping tea in Mrs. Bower's kitchen, Lillian unable to express her sorrow in words, yet thankful for the company. Mrs. Bower's presence had seemed to exude peace in the midst of Lillian's storm and helped relieve a small portion of the crushing loneliness that threatened to drown her at every turn.

Mrs. Bower was loved and respected by all, a woman of thoughtfulness and charity who valued people over possessions. She was active in the church, teaching the women's Sunday School class every week without fail. Her late husband's lumber business, in addition to providing her with untold wealth, had given her the means to help those less fortunate in Waverly, and her reputation for serving others was legendary.

And yet, to Lillian, she was all of this and so much more. She was proof. Mrs. Bower threw a lifeline of friendship to Lillian when she was sinking into despair and shown her tangible proof that it was possible to go on living, despite losing half your soul.

"Ma'am, there's something else," Mitchell said, and the torrent of memories disappeared as quickly as it had come.

Something else? Lillian couldn't form the words to ask him what else there could possibly be, so she waited.

"Mr. Smith said Doc Baker told him..." Mitchell swallowed and looked down again, his cheeks flushed. "Well, apparently, she had been … violated, ma'am."

Lillian stared at him in horror, her hand involuntarily covering her mouth as a rush of bile threatened to bubble up from her gut. She stood up, her legs shaking, and stepped to the window. "Who could do such a thing?" she whispered, wishing she could wake up from this nightmare.

Mitchell's voice sounded far away. "It was terrible, ma'am. I mean, from what Doc Baker and the neighbors said. Just terrible."

Lillian pressed her forehead against the smooth glass and gulped for air. She felt as if she were drowning, or as if an unrelenting, heavy stone was pushing down on her chest. She was suddenly afraid to open her mouth to speak, fearing a wail of anguish might escape.

She was vaguely aware of Mitchell's voice in the background. "I can't believe something like this could happen in Waverly. And to such a sweet old lady, too. Whoever did this must be some kind of monster."

A monster.

A searing memory flashed through her mind, a memory of listening to a hushed conversation from the doorway of four-year-old Mary's room. Everett, sitting on the edge of the little bed, patiently promising a terrified Mary for the fifth time that night that there were no scary monsters under her bed. He even went so far as to get on the floor and wiggle his upper body underneath the bed as far as he could go just to prove it. "You're safe," he had whispered, smoothing back her hair. "There's nothing to be scared of. Daddy's right here, and I won't let anything happen to you."

But now, Everett was gone, and Lillian knew without a doubt that some monsters are real.

CHAPTER NINE - DANIEL

June 7, 1936

Daniel knocked on the door and then put his hands in his pockets, whistling softly and glancing left and right, trying to look like he was simply out for a casual Sunday stroll. Sweat trickled down his forehead, and he wiped it from his brow before it made its way into his eyes. He moved slightly to the left to stand in the shade, not that it made much difference in this blazing heat, and leaned against the building, hoping to relieve some of the pressure from his aching foot.

He knocked again on the thick door, thinking maybe she hadn't heard him from her tiny room above the tavern. His fear increased with every second that slowly ticked by. The past few hours had found him swinging dizzily from shock, to sheer panic at the thought of the police questioning him, to absolute confidence that he was safe, and back to sheer terror again. He'd done his best to cover his tracks, but he felt exposed, like an injured animal in an open field. He hated being in this situation and he hated the tangled blanket of fear that was suffocating him, but most of all, he hated feeling powerless.

He frantically tried to think of an excuse in case someone came walking by, a logical reason to be in this alley, knocking on the tavern's back door on a Sunday morning. He counted to ten, figuring if she didn't come to the door soon, he would keep walking. He would sneak back to his room to retrieve a few meager belongings, then hide out for a couple of days until he could send a letter to his sister back in Virginia.

He reached the number ten and turned to go, deciding he couldn't wait any longer, when he heard a soft click and the heavy door opened a tiny crack. Sally's beautiful, chocolate brown eyes peered out at him, and he couldn't help but smile.

She didn’t return his smile. Instead, her face showed only confusion as she wrapped her thin cotton robe a little tighter around herself and smoothed her frizzy hair back away from her face.

"Daniel, what're you doin' here? Hershel ain't gonna be happy if he catches you sneakin' 'round here like this. You know how he feels about you."

His smile vanished as quickly as it had appeared. Of course he was being careful, that's why he came to the back door. Did she honestly think he was that stupid?

He took a deep breath, fighting to control his temper.

"Sally, I need a favor, but I can't exactly tell you why." He glanced over his shoulder and then looked back at her. "If you're willin' to help me, that is." He spoke in low tones and searched her eyes, trying to keep the desperation out of his voice while also trying to convey the urgency of the situation. It was a fine balancing act.

She opened the door wider. "Daniel, are you in some kinda trouble?" Before he even opened his mouth to answer, she stepped closer and continued in a quick whisper, the words tumbling out. "I heard a commotion early this mornin' and stepped out front, and there was a whole mess of people makin' their way down to ol' Lady Bower's place." She nodded in the direction of the house a few blocks down the street. "I asked Hershel, and he said all kinds o' folks been goin' in and out over there all mornin'." She stopped suddenly and turned her head, peering at his face. "What's goin' on?"

He tried to control his breathing. He was glad they were at the back door, away from the crowd gathered down the street. There was no way he'd be able to makc it back to his room without being seen now, not with it being so close to the Bower house.

"Doll, I ... I didn't know where else to go," he said. "I need your help." He wiped the never-ending sweat from his brow and licked his lips and tried desperately to figure out the best way to explain this impossible situation.

She searched his face, waiting.

"Sally, I was wonderin' if maybe I could stay here with you, just for a little while. I reckon I'm in a bit of a jam." He looked down, feigning embarrassment as the lies came tumbling out. "The truth is, I ain't got my rent money again, and Emmett's not gonna give me a break this time. I need to get things caught up, and I've gotta stay away from him 'til I do."

"Baby, you know you can't stay here. Hershel would never allow it." He frowned and shook his head, but she continued anyway, putting her hand gently on the side of his face. "Listen, I prob'ly got enough put back to pay Emmett. Just give me a minute to fetch it."

As she turned to go, he grabbed her arm, his grip like a vise.

"No, Sally. I ain't takin' money from you, not again. If Emmett sees me 'round, he's gonna call the law. I gots to lay low right now. Just for a few days."

"Daniel, you're hurting me," she said in a quiet voice, squirming.

"I'm sorry, doll, I'm so sorry." He loosened his grip and stared down at the hand that seemed somehow detached from his body. This wasn't working. He heard a door slam down the block and glanced back over his shoulder, his heart hammering. What if someone saw him talking to her in this alley? He didn't have a clue what he'd say at this point. He needed time to think, to get his story straight before word got out.

He tried again. "Look, Sally, I need you. I ain't got nobody else." He stared directly into her dark eyes, willing her to say yes, willing his heart to slow its incessant pounding. He felt exposed, panicked, a sickening sense of desperation and helplessness crowding out all other thoughts. He found himself questioning everything - his carefully laid plans, his ability to escape, and now even Sally's loyalty.

What if this whole thing had been a terrible mistake?

"Please," he whispered. "Don't make me beg."

She stared at him for just a moment before her eyes widened and she took a small step back. "Daniel, what happened? What did you do?"

His face hardened at the suspicion in her eyes before he could even fully registered her words.

What did you do?

That's all she could say?

He should have known better than to come here. She was like everyone else in this god-forsaken town. So quick to blame him, so quick to assume he was trouble, so quick to accuse. It didn't matter if he tried to explain, so why bother? She would never believe him. None of them would.

"You know what? Just forget it." He spat the words out as he turned to go. She reached out to grab his arm, but he shrugged her off. He walked around the corner and continued down the alley, ignoring her apology and her frantic pleas for him to come back.

He cut through the alley, turned right, walked a couple of blocks further, and then turned right again on Crittenden Street. He stopped at the mill company to take advantage of the shade under the building's red awning, his shirt clinging uncomfortably to his back. He gazed down the street, his heart thumping wildly at the sight of the large crowd gathered in the yard up the street. He couldn't make out what anyone was saying. He did, however, notice a big black car pull up in front of the Bower house, and his muscles tensed when Sheriff Lillian Conner climbed out of it.

He turned and began walking quickly back the way he had came, retracing his steps, south on 2nd Street, toward Thomason's Department Store.

How long would it be before they came looking for him? He wiped rivulets of sweat away from his forehead as he passed Anderson's grocery, huge block letters in the window announcing a sale on produce. The downtown streets were nearly deserted, as they were on most Sundays, the businesses closed up tight, their interiors darkened and deserted. He caught a glimpse of his wide eyes and frantic expression reflecting back at him from a store window. He needed to calm the hell down. He forced himself to stop, take a few deep breaths, and straighten his shirt collar.

No one saw him climb out the old lady's window, of that, he was sure. He had slipped right out and vanished into the darkened street, quick as a hot knife through butter.

But he couldn't keep walking forever, especially with the ache in his sore foot. And if Sally assumed he was involved in what happened, he knew everyone else would, too. He needed to get out of town. Fast.

CHAPTER TEN - SARAH

June 16, 2006

I sat up with a start, clutching the blankets, sure that my terror was palpable in the room, that my pounding heart had been loud enough to wake Steve. I fought to slow my breathing, then stretched and rolled my shoulders to release the tension from the muscles in my neck. With a glance of jealousy at my husband who was snoring softly, I shuffled across the darkened room to the door and headed downstairs to put a kettle on for some tea.

It had been one of those dreams that seemed so vivid, so incredibly detailed, my brain struggled to separate reality from the terrifying images my subconscious had produced. Flashes of it replayed in my mind like a horror movie I couldn't stop watching.

The first things I noticed were the sounds.

Crickets chirped in the fields, and Granny Patsy's hydrangeas seemed to whisper as they shivered in the breeze. I carried a flashlight, the white beam of light cutting through the blanket of darkness directly in front of me. I was inexplicably barefoot, the dew-dampened grass tickling my feet. I walked purposefully, one hand clutching my flashlight, the other rubbing carefully along the smoothness of the aluminum siding. An unidentifiable noise came from within the house, perhaps a voice, though the message was unclear. I walked a few steps and then noticed it again, my ears straining to make out the words. I couldn't understand what was being said, but I felt an overwhelming sense of urgency to get inside the house, to find the source of this mysterious voice. I quickened my pace and stumbled a bit on the wet lawn, but when I turned the corner, I stopped, confused. This should be the front of the property, but where was the porch? Where was the front door? I glanced around, the flashlight producing only a pinprick of light in the enveloping darkness. I saw the sidewalk leading up to the house through the veil of darkness, and yet the cracked concrete pathway did not end at the front porch steps, as I knew without a doubt that it should. Instead, it simply disappeared into the foundation beneath the house.

I stared in confusion until I again heard the faint voice coming from inside. I stood perfectly still, holding my breath, all my senses focused on the sound. I stepped closer and pressed my ear against the side of the house. The hairs on the back of my neck stood at attention as I made out one word coming from within.

Sarah.

The voice sounded like a whisper, so soft it could have been only the wind. A moment later, I caught it again.

Sarah.

I ran along the side of the house and turned the corner, but I saw only the same white aluminum siding stretching out in front of me. I ran to the end and turned another corner, to what should have been the back of the house. The back porch was nowhere to be found.

My terror grew as the voice repeated my name, much louder now.

Sarah... Sarah ....

The sound was a funeral dirge emanating from within the ancient walls of the farmhouse, and I knew I had to find a way inside.

My heart raced as I ran, turned a corner, ran, turned a corner, ran, turned a corner, each time finding only an endless purgatory of white, aluminum stretching before me.

A sharp stab of pain shot through my knee as I stumbled in the dewy grass and fell on the sidewalk. I crouched there, my breath ragged and gasping, my wild eyes searching for an entrance.

Sarah.... Sarah...

There had to be a way to get in, a window, a door, something.

I registered movement across the yard by the huge oak tree near the barn. Peering into the darkness, I directed the flashlight towards the tree with the tire swing where I spent countless hours playing as a child. Only this time, there was no tire swing. Instead, the shadowy form of a corpse was hanging from a noose tied to a low branch.

The horrifying sight of the figure twisting gently in the breeze shocked my subconscious enough to allow me to escape back to the sanctuary of my bedroom, my husband sleeping peacefully beside me.

In an effort to calm my nerves and forget about the terrifying dream, I turned on every light downstairs, poured a mug of soothing tea, and settled in with the Legal Ethics textbook I had been avoiding for days. I needed to finish this week's reading assignment and discussion board questions for my online class, and if anything could slow down my racing heart, this would do it.

I opened the textbook with a sigh, but my wandering eyes were soon drawn to the stacks of old newspaper articles spread out on the coffee table in front of me. I tried again to focus, but the screaming headlines and grainy, old photographs called out to me, demanding my attention. I realized this was a battle I couldn't win. I tossed the book aside, picked a page at random, and began reading.

"What on earth are you doing?" Steve yawned and shuffled over to sit on the couch beside me.

"I couldn't sleep, so I decided to make some tea and do a little reading," I said.

He leaned over and picked up a page with an article written two days after the murder. He sat back on the couch and skimmed the text.

"I can't believe your grandfather actually witnessed this," he said. "I mean, can you imagine? This was a huge deal."

"I know, and now he doesn't want to talk about it. I want so badly to ask him what it was really like, but he just won't budge." I shook my head in wonder.

"Why do you think he keeps shutting you down?" he asked.

"I'm not sure. I mean, he brought the whole thing up to me to start with. I feel like he wanted to talk about it at first, but now he's almost sorry he mentioned it."

Steve placed the article back on the table, stood, and stretched his long arms overhead. "Well, Detective Harper, I'm sure you'll get to the bottom of it soon," he said. "I'm going to head up to shower. I need to finish my presentation today and make some calls to finalize things before this trip." He bent to give me a quick peck on the cheek.

"Okay. What time's your flight tomorrow? I know you told me last night, but I think I was already half gone when you said it."

"That's okay, I'm used to you falling asleep mid-conversation." He winked as I stuck my tongue out at him. "Flight leaves at 8am. I'll be working late tonight getting things wrapped up at the office, so if you want to go visit your Grandaddy for a bit after work, that would be totally cool. It might be good for you to try again to talk to him about all of this," he said as he waved a hand over the coffee table.

"Thanks. I think I might do that."

A few minutes later, I heard Steve turn on the shower upstairs. I flipped through the articles, gathering them into a pile with a sigh. As I slid them back into the folder, I noticed a story from the day after the murder. I wondered briefly what those first few days must have been like, when the police were searching for a vicious murderer on the loose in Waverly. I could only imagine the fear that must have gripped the town. I thought about Daniel Porter, hiding out in those first few days, knowing his life was over if they caught him. I pictured Sheriff Conner, the weight of responsibility she must have felt to capture the murderer and keep the citizens safe. And I tried to imagine my grandfather as a young man, watching it all.

CHAPTER ELEVEN - SALLY

June 7, 1936

The first thing she noticed was the sound.

It was like the wind rustling through leaves, or the dangerous low rumble of a hornet's nest. Voices blending, feet shuffling on the sidewalk, people shifting in the blazing sunlight. Eyes peered over shoulders to try and get a better view of the house on the corner. It was still early in the day, but the humidity made the air thick and still, and so many bodies in one area certainly did nothing to relieve the oppressive heat. Some stood by the front porch, others gathered in the yard to the side of the steps, as if afraid to get too close, yet worried they would miss something if they moved farther away.

She cautiously approached the outskirts of the crowd, listening for snatches of conversation from the onlookers, but all she heard were mumblings and whispers. It reminded her of slow nights at Tiegg's, when a handful of customers sipped their drinks and carried on hushed conversations.

She hunted for a familiar face among the group. Finding none, she pressed forward, straining to see.

A shiver of excitement traveled through the crowd when the front door opened and Sheriff Conner stepped out on the porch. She seemed hesitant, as if unsure whether to make a statement or keep walking. Several men in the front tipped their hats at her, and she nodded back. She smoothed down her dress, adjusted her handbag on her forearm, and turned to speak to one of the young officers who had been standing guard by the door. Sally strained to hear them, but she could not catch even a word of what was being said. The officer followed as Sheriff Conner stepped off the porch and walked towards the waiting black Ford.

A tall white man who had been at the front crossed in front of Sally. She didn't want to know, and yet her mouth opened and the words came tumbling out anyway. "Excuse me, sir. Could you tell me what's happening?"

The man looked down at her and shook his head in disgust before pushing past her and continuing across the street.

She turned away, embarrassed. Waverly was full of neighborly folks who treated blacks with kindness, but sometimes she forgot that not everyone felt that way.

Her eyes fell on Sam Campbell, a regular at the tavern, standing nearby. He was fanning himself with his hat, and to his credit, he continued gazing straight ahead, as if he had not seen the white man's rudeness.

The front door opened again, and she watched as a grim-faced man with a black leather satchel stepped out of the house. He frowned and shook his head as he closed the door behind him, then walked down the steps and began making his way to a car waiting down the block.

"Sam, who's that? The doctor?" she asked.

Sam glanced around furtively before whispering back, "That was no doctor. That there was Mister Robert Clayton. He's the coroner."

Her voice came out in a frantic whisper, questions tumbling over one another even though she already knew the answers. "The coroner? What happened? What's he doing here?"

The world seemed to spin around her. The sky, trees, buildings, people, houses, and the ground all became a blur.

"Miss Sally, are you okay?"

She swayed on her feet, gulping air and yet unable to catch her breath. Sam grabbed her elbow to steady her. She fanned her face with her hand, desperate for a cool breeze, anything to relieve the relentless fire burning within and without. Why was it so blasted hot?

"Miss Sally?" Sam's voice grew louder with concern. He sounded far away, like she was underwater and he was calling down to her through the depths.

The crowd of white folks shifted to face her, aware of a disturbance in their midst. She glanced around at the white faces surrounding her, unfriendly faces dripping with disgust and annoyance. She tried to tell them she just needed a minute to catch her breath, but her vocal cords were frozen, her tongue glued firmly to the roof of her mouth.

What was happening? What was happening?

Hershel appeared beside her and gripped her arm in almost the same spot where Daniel had grabbed her that morning, inadvertently squeezing the purplish bruise that was forming beneath her dress sleeve. The flash of pain snapped her back to her senses.

She shook her head, swallowed, and gently removed Hershel's hand from her arm. "I'm fine, I'm fine. Thank you. It's this heat, that's all."

The crowd murmured, satisfied, and shifted its focus away from her, back to the porch.

A deputy stood on the porch and addressed the crowd. "Gentlemen, we're gonna have to ask you to move along now. This here is a crime scene, and we have a lot of serious work to do."

A rumble of excitement traveled through the onlookers like a wave as they began to disperse.

"I'm not sure what happened," Sam said in a low voice as he turned to Sally and Hershel, his eyes wide. "But there's only one reason they'd fetch the coroner."

Images of Daniel's hardened, angry face as he had walked away from her in the alley earlier that morning flashed through Sally's mind, along with the echo of her last words to him. "*Daniel, what happened? What did you do?*"

PART 2

THE INVESTIGATION

CHAPTER TWELVE - LILLIAN

June 7, 1936

Robert Clayton, the county coroner, took his glasses off and wiped them with a handkerchief. "It's not good, Sheriff. Not good at all."

Doc Baker nodded in agreement, setting his glass of water on the desk. "I agree. Terrible shame."

Their words hung in the air for a moment before Lillian cleared her throat. "Yes, well, I suppose we need to start by reviewing the facts," she said. She took a sip of strong black coffee, hoping the men wouldn't notice her hand shaking. What she saw in Mrs. Bower's bedroom that morning had produced a persistent quaking that seemed to come from the very marrow of her bones.

Lillian picked up her pen and stared at the blank piece of paper in front of her. She knew she should take notes but was unsure of what to write at the top of the page. *Crime Scene Details*? *Notes on the Death of Mrs. Bower*? *Murder Investigation*? She wondered briefly if there was a form she should be using somewhere in the ancient filing cabinet in the corner, or if this simple sheet of paper would do.

"This was a violent crime, no doubt about that," Doc Baker said, interrupting her thoughts. "We'll need an autopsy to confirm cause of death, of course, but I'd say it's a fair bet the victim was killed by strangulation."

Lillian wrote *Interview with Doc Baker and Coroner Clayton* at the top of the blank piece of paper. She followed this with the words *strangled to death.*

"Well now, I would say the discoloration and swelling around her neck certainly indicate manual strangulation," Clayton agreed, "but she also received several blows to the head. Hard to say at this point if she was beaten and knocked unconscious before being choked, or if it was the other way around. We won't know for sure until we've examined her further."

"True, true," Doc Baker conceded.

"I see. And was she rendered unconscious before..." Lillian trailed off, her voice failing her.

"You mean before she was violated?" Clayton asked.

Lillian swallowed and nodded, staring down at the paper in front of her. Out of the corner of her eye, she saw him glance at Doc Baker before answering.

"Well, if injuries are sustained after death, there is little to no bruising at all," the coroner said gently. "Unfortunately, the markings on her body indicate she was conscious during most of the assault."

"I agree," Doc Baker added. "I noticed she had quite a bit of redness and swelling on her head, face, and neck. We won't really know the full extent of her injuries until we examine her further, but I cannot stress to you enough that this was a vicious, vicious attack, Sheriff Conner. I've not seen anything like it in my thirty years of practicing medicine."

"I concur," Doc Baker said grimly. "The sheets and the victim's gown, which was still pulled up above her waist, were both covered in a large amount of blood."

Lillian concentrated on the mechanics of writing, carefully forming each word on the page. She tried to convince herself the words she wrote, words like *strangled* and *blood on sheets*, were in fact no more than a group of meaningless, connected letters flowing in looping cursive across the page. They were not details of a real event, not a description of what had happened in that bedroom down the street, not a narrative of a brutal attack on a kind and gentle woman who had been her friend.

"Do you know what time it happened?" Lillian asked, swallowing down the bile that had risen in her throat.

"Well, based on the body's condition, it must have been sometime last night or early this morning. What do you think, Robert?"

Clayton nodded. "She shows early signs of rigor mortis, so most likely within the past six to twelve hours."

Lillian nodded and looked down at the paper in front of her, adding the estimated time of death to her notes. She looked up and saw the men glancing at each other and then back at her. The doubt and pity in their eyes was unmistakable.

"Well, I thank you both for your time," she said with a sigh. "I suppose I need to share this information with my men so we can continue with our investigation. We have some anxious neighbors waiting to be interviewed."

The men stood to go as she continued, "Thank you again for agreeing to meet me here, by the way. I'm not sure how these things are normally done, but I could not stand the thought of discussing the details with you at the house. The street was full of neighbors, and that was no place to talk about things like this."

Doc Baker nodded, "Understandable, ma'am. You made the right decision for sure."

With a weary sigh, she closed the office door behind them, turned, and stood with her back against it. She felt as if she were all alone, floating atop a small raft in the middle of a sea of emotions, being battered by a storm. Every wave threatened to toss her right over the edge, to send her flailing into the depths where she might be swallowed up forever. She longed to be somewhere else, to be someone else. Someone who didn't carry the responsibility of dealing with a gruesome event like this.

Somehow, the killer's method added an intimacy to the crime that made Lillian's skin crawl. A murderer in a rage could fire a gun from across the room and never get close to his victim. The victim was no less dead, the murderer no less guilty. But to intimately violate a woman and then squeeze the very life out of her with your own hands? She shuddered. It required a familiarity and a closeness that made the crime all the more horrific.

She tried to imagine Everett handling this investigation. Calm, steady Everett. He would have known exactly what to do to find the killer and keep Waverly safe.

And he would have kept it all to himself, made sure to spare her of the grisly details.

A rush of voices met her as soon as she opened the door and stepped into the hall.

"Do you have any leads, sheriff?"

"Did you talk to Delbert Moore yet? I'll bet he heard something..."

"We have two boxes of evidence already logged, ma'am..."

"I seen a couple of colored boys hangin' 'round downtown after dark..."

Lillian raised a hand to silence the storm of voices. In what she hoped was an authoritative voice, she turned to Deputy Stone and instructed, "I need you and Deputy Johnston to take statements from the neighbors while Mitchell and I go over the evidence." Ignoring the questioning stares of those gathered in the hall, she moved past them and walked purposefully into the spare office, which had been converted into a makeshift evidence room. Mitchell followed behind her.

She closed the door firmly before turning to face the deputy. "Mitchell, I cannot begin to fathom what is going to be required of me here," she began. "But our foremost priority must be to find the person who did this."

Mitchell nodded, but before he could speak, Lillian said, “I've done my best to take on Everett's role here at the station these last four months." The constant dull ache in her heart grew stronger at the very mention of his name. "It’s no secret I’m out of my element here. As my senior deputy, I’m going to be leaning on you to help me with this. I fully understand that many in town doubt about my ability to carry out the duties of this office, but we must be careful to make sure any doubts about my qualifications do not hinder this case."

"Ma'am, you know how much I admired your husband," the young deputy said seriously. "He was a fine man, and I realize how difficult this transition has been for you. For all of us. But I promise I will do everything in my power to help you find the monster who did this and see that justice is served."

Lillian nodded and managed a small smile before turning to open the first box of evidence. “So, where do we start?”

"Okay, so, we removed items we thought might pertain to the crime and documented them on this sheet," Mitchell said. He handed her a ledger page. "It lists a description of the item, as well as where it was found and by whom."

Her eyes scanned down the list as Mitchell began removing items from the box. "It says here that a man's ring was found at the scene, but there was certainly no man living with Mrs. Bower. Any idea who it belongs to?"

"No, we haven't figured that out yet."

"Was it found with her jewelry?"

"No. Her jewelry box was empty, but I found the ring on a side table in the bedroom. It looks cheap, maybe even homemade. Seemed mighty peculiar to me."

"Wait. Surely you don't think the criminal left it there?" Lillian asked, incredulous.

"Well, I doubt that. I mean, what kind of murderer would be that careless?" He shrugged and began removing other items from the evidence box, lining them up on the table. "It's probably nothing."

Lillian nodded absently and peered at the ring. She could just make out a crude letter D carved into the band. She tilted it in the light, hoping to get a better view, then shrugged and put it on the table. Mitchell was right. It was probably nothing.

CHAPTER THIRTEEN - SARAH

June 19, 2006

"Hey, you got a second?"

Mark looked up from his laptop and took off his glasses. "Of course. Everything okay?"

I walked in and sat in the chair across from him, already feeling guilty about pulling him away from the piles of notes and documents scattered over his desk.

"Look, this is going to sound strange," I began. "I know we're up to our eyeballs in work preparing for this case and everything, but I wanted to pick your brain about something totally off topic."

"Sure, I need a break from this anyway." He smiled curiously. "So, what's on your mind?"

I took a deep breath. "Do you know anything about a guy named Daniel Porter?"

He frowned. "Daniel Porter? That name sounds vaguely familiar."

"He was the last person publicly executed in the United States. It happened right here in Waverly, actually."

"Oh, that's right. I read about that." He nodded.

"Well, I'm doing a research paper for one of my classes, and I've been studying the Porter case."

"Pretty wild story, from what I remember."

"Yeah, it is. Look, I know this sounds weird, but I kind of have a vested interest, besides just the research paper. It seems my grandfather witnessed the execution." I shrugged. "Well, I mean, I think he did, anyway."

"Wow! No kidding?"

"Yeah, I had no idea any of this had happened in Waverly, and certainly no idea my grandfather was there. He mentioned it a few days ago. but now he doesn't want to talk about it."

"Really?"

"Yeah, he totally changed the subject. Told me it happened a long time ago and we should just leave it in the past."

"Well, can you blame him?"

I looked back at him in silence, unable to hide my confusion.

"Sarah, he's been living with those memories for all of these years, and he's an old man. He must be, what, in his nineties by now, right?" He shrugged. "Maybe he just doesn't want to think about things like that."

"I would think after seventy years he'd at least be able to talk about it, though." I paused, unsure whether I should continue.

"What?" he prompted.

"Well, honestly, I can't help but wonder if he was more... involved somehow."

"What do you mean, 'involved'?"

"I'm not exactly sure. Maybe he knew the victim or someone close to the case or something."

"Hmmm... could be," he said carefully.

"I went to the library and pulled some of the newspaper articles from that summer, but it's impossible to tell if what I'm reading is actually how it happened, you know?" I gave him my most hopeful smile. "Anyway, I was wondering if maybe I could get access to the trial transcripts."

"Seriously?" he asked.

"Yes, seriously. I have no idea how to track down court transcripts from seventy years ago, but I'm sure you do." I realized he was frowning. "Look, I realize how crazy this sounds, but I need to know what happened."

"Sarah, I'm not sure this is such a good idea.

"Why not?"

"Well, we all know you've been under a lot of pressure lately," he said. When I didn't respond, he continued, "Look, I'm just worried about you. You've been through a lot these past few months, with everything that happened."

I felt my cheeks flush. "Mark, I told you before, I'm fine," I said evenly.

"Of course you are." His words poured out in a rush. "You're under a lot of stress, though, with this trial coming up and your grad classes and everything, and I still don't think you gave yourself enough time off after what happened. You need to grieve, Sarah, to let yourself heal, inside and out. I don't think obsessing about this case is the best thing for you right now."

"I am not obsessing." Even as the words left my mouth, I knew I was lying. "And my condition is none of your concern." I hated the cold, flat tone of my voice, but even more, I hated him for making me sound that way.

He stared quietly at the desk between us, and a sudden torrent of guilt washed over me.

"Mark, I'm sorry. I appreciate you worrying about me." I softened my tone and forced a small smile. "I'm fine, and I promise, I'm not obsessing. I just want to understand what happened."

He shrugged. "Okay, fine. Let me call Deborah over at the courthouse. She can probably contact someone over in Louisville at the Judicial Center's Law Library and help us figure out where to start."

Relief flooded over me. "Thanks so much, Mark."

"No problem. In fact, I'll go ahead and call Deborah now, while I'm thinking about it. I'll also try and get you Frank Sims' number. He took over as county prosecutor in the 1950s. He spends most of his time now fishing out at Panther Creek, but he might be willing to give you some insight."

"That would be awesome," I said as I stood to go. "I really appreciate your help with this."

"Sure thing," he smiled.

As I turned to leave, he said, "Sarah, I wasn't kidding earlier. You need to take care of yourself, okay?"

"I will. I'm heading out to lunch now, but I'll leave the machine on, so don't worry about the phones," I said.

"Okay, thanks," he said, and then turned his attention back to the stacks of papers on his desk.

Five minutes later, I found myself parked in an empty parking space at the corner of 5th and Crittenden, staring at an old house. The boarded up windows stared back at me, as if challenging me to unlock the secrets they held. I tried to imagine this crumbling structure in 1936, back when it was a stately home with a porch that didn't sag and paint that hadn't flaked away. I pictured the neighbors and onlookers gathered in the front yard, a crowd of people whispering and speculating about what might have happened to the Widow Bower in that house. Goosebumps appeared on my arms as I wondered if my grandfather had been among them.

CHAPTER FOURTEEN - DANIEL

June 8, 1936

Daniel delicately peeled back the layers of orange rind and inhaled the sweet smell of citrus. He popped a small slice in his mouth and savored the intoxicating juices. He'd managed to swipe a couple of pieces of fruit from the display in front of Pearson's grocery that morning and high-tail it back down to the river without being seen. Now, his stomach roared, and it took every ounce of his willpower to keep from devouring the fruit whole.

He had counted on staying with Sally for awhile, which meant finding food would be no trouble at all. But much like the rest of his plans, that part failed miserably. No telling when he'd have a chance to eat again.

He placed another dripping slice of orange in his mouth and studied his surroundings. The detectives must be hard at work by now. Mrs. Bower was a widow, and more importantly, a rich, white widow. He was lucky to find this shed at the edge of town when he did. It looked like a stiff breeze would easily send its weathered, slanting walls crashing down around him, but the slope of the riverbank and the crop of trees nearby provided an adequate screen from the road. The open door allowed for a welcome breeze, although the air was still hot and muggy. The shed was a safe haven, a refuge that provided him with a tiny flicker of hope that he might still make it out of this mess, despite his failed plans. Within these timeworn walls, he could breathe, had a place to think, was safe. At least, as safe as he could be, given the circumstances.

Daniel stood in the doorway and looked out over the water. The muddy Ohio was by no means a beauty, but all the same, he appreciated the peaceful view. The occasional log or branch peeked above the waterline, carried smoothly downriver by the brown water. He tried to judge the speed of the current and wondered, not for the first time, about his chances of swimming across to the Indiana side. He figured it was no more than a half mile across, but he was by no means a good swimmer, and even if he made it, folks at the fishing camp on the other side would be mighty curious to see a black man covered in mud crawling up the river banks.

He looked around and took stock of the items in the shed, though he had done so at least a hundred times the day before. The shed was a cemetery of rusted equipment and damaged, broken things. He wondered briefly who owned the ancient building. Maybe some old tinkerer in town, a collector of junk with good intentions, but no follow-through.

When he had first walked in, he had discovered an old fishing pole and laughed out loud at the unexpected stroke of good luck. It wasn't until he pulled the pole out for a closer look that he noticed the broken shaft and missing line.

He looked over at the stack of rusted metal buckets sitting in one corner beside an old metal rake, the tines broken and bent. A large hammer with a busted handle leaned against an ancient two-bottom plow, which took up most of the floor space. One of the plow wheels had simply vanished, while the other rested at a crazy angle. The whole contraption leaned dangerously to the left, the plow heads having sunk several inches into the dirt floor. Random slats of wood in various sizes were also scattered about the room and filled a rusted horse trough by the door. Small, unidentifiable scraps of metal and pebbles littered the floor. He used the broken rake the night before to scrape most of the debris out of the way. Hidden fragments still poked painfully into his back as he slept, as if to remind him nothing, including sleep, would come easy from here on out.

He ran through his plans again, ticking off the steps one by one. He needed to remove the jewelry from Frank Newell's barn as quickly as possible. If he hitched a ride to Louisville and sold the jewels, he figured he'd have more than enough to buy a train ticket to Roanoke. From there, his sister's husband, John, could meet him at the train station and take him back to their house. Easy peasy, if not for one tiny complication. Daniel had nearly killed John the last time they'd seen each other.

He looked down at the ground and shook his head, remembering his last night on the small cot in the back room of their house in Virginia. Through the wall, he had heard Ruth hiss, "Keep your voice down, John, please," but she needn't have bothered. Daniel had put his hands tightly over his ears and buried his head beneath his pillow, but he still heard every word. He had gathered the soft old quilt on his cot up into a ball and pounded his fist into it over, and over, in rhythm to his brother-in-law's booming voice coming through the thin wall.

"He's a grown man, Ruth. Why we feedin' and lookin' after him like he's still a child? I'm gettin' sick and tired of him layin' 'round here like king of the castle, not doin' a damn thing to earn his keep. If you won't tell him to get out, I'm fixin' to do it myself..."

Daniel fumed to hear his sister begging John to listen. Begging, as if she had no say in it, as if she had no choice but to turn her back on her own flesh and blood.

There was a crash and a thud against the wall, and then a muffled scream. Daniel threw open the door and saw his sister, his sweet Ruth, her eyes wide as she frantically clawed at John's fingers, squeezing around her neck like a vise.

Daniel was across the room in two strides, knocking John to the floor, pounding his fists against him, over and over, like he had pounded the balled up quilt just moments before. He blocked out the sound of Ruth gulping in lungfuls of air behind him and focused only on slamming his fists into John's nose, his anger exploding through his knuckles, now slick with blood, pounding and pounding against the bloody pulp that had been John's face. And then he ran. He ran out the door and down the road, not daring to look back, leaving his weeping sister behind to clean up the mess.

Seeing Ruth's fear that night had released something white hot inside of him, like molten lava, something he was powerless to stop, even if he had wanted to. But he hadn't wanted to, not really. Deep down, he wanted to hurt John, had enjoyed making him pay, wanted him to know the same fear he had unleashed in Ruth.

It seemed like such a long, long time ago, and so much had happened since then. But Ruth would still need some time to convince John to let him come home, and it wouldn't be easy. As risky as it was, Daniel would have to get someone to help him send her a letter. He knew his sister would welcome him back like always, but he had no intentions of being greeted by the business end of her husband's shotgun.

CHAPTER FIFTEEN - SALLY

June 9, 1936

She was shaking out the rugs in the alley when she saw him sneaking furtively around the corner. He kept his head down, his hat pulled low over his forehead despite the heat, but she would recognize him anywhere. He moved with a sort of graceful motion that matched his delicate, compact stature, so unlike the rough farmers and coal miners she grew up around in Rhea County. But as she watched more closely, she realized something looked off. She saw he was favoring one leg over the other, each step of his normally smooth stride ending with a little shuffle that wasn't normally there.

He stopped in front of her and dropped a canvas bundle on the ground by his feet. He gently put his warm hands over hers so they held the blue and gray rug suspended between them. Sally imagined it was a line that could not be crossed. All the words she had planned to say if she ever saw him again became lodged in her throat, and she stared into his brown eyes, wondering where to begin.

"Sally, I'm sorry for leaving you standin' there like that the other day. I just didn't know what else to do."

She swallowed and looked at him, a tangle of emotions coursing through her.

"The truth is," he continued in a soft voice, glancing down for a moment before again meeting her gaze, "I lied, Sally. To my ever-lastin' shame, I lied to you. I told you I needed a place to stay for a few days 'cause I ain't got no rent money, but that ain't the truth at all."

She stared at him, her eyes widening.

"The truth is, there's people here in town who're gonna blame me for what happened to the Widow Bower," he murmured, shrugging his shoulders. "But, Sally, you know I ain't got nothin' to do with all that. I'd never hurt nobody, not really."

She nodded her head slowly. She did know that about him. Didn't she?

"I got no reason to kill that ol' lady, but the police ain't gonna listen to me. Naw, they'll come askin' me questions, and if they don't like my answers, it'll be all over for me. They hang people for murder, Sally. Especially people like me." He shook his head. "I ain't got a chance in hell."

It made sense. It honestly did. She knew it as well as anybody, and had known it her whole life. Her daddy taught her from an early age that life wasn't fair, would never be fair, but you still gave it everything you got, fought with every ounce of energy you could muster. After her mama died, though, things changed. It was like the fight went right out of him. He spent the next ten years staring into the bottom of glass, trying to drown his memories and that part of himself that was too painful to face, all while telling her she had to work twice as hard as anyone if she ever wanted to get somewhere in life. Sally thought her daddy was a hypocrite of the worst kind, quick to speak, but slow to act. He yelled about the high and mighty white folks in town and how Sally needed to rise up when the world tried to keep her down, but he never seemed to claw up that hill himself. He was a flag bearer, quick to rally the troops and charge them to battle, but never picking up a gun.

She thought back to when she first arrived in Waverly, how she expected things to be different, and how bitterly disappointed she was to find that they weren't. Hatred and suspicion were everywhere, and no matter how hard she worked, her skin was a prison she could never escape.

"Daniel, I am so sorry I ever doubted you." Tears filled her eyes, but she would not draw her hand away from Daniel's to wipe them.

"You was just scared." He shrugged and offered her a small smile. "Don't cry, now, doll. You know I can't stand to see them pretty eyes cryin'."

She took a deep, quivering breath and nodded.

He chewed his bottom lip for a moment and said, "I hate to ask, darlin', but I got nowheres else to go. I need you to do somethin' for me."

"Of course, Daniel. Anything." And she meant it.

He smiled again and said, "Good. Truth is, I'm fixin' to go back home, Sally. Back to Virginia."

The air rushed from her lungs. She understood he needed to stay out of sight until things calmed down. But *Virginia?*

"Sally, you know how the people in this town are. Ever time somethin' happens, it's gonna be like this. I'll always be on the run, or tryin' to prove myself." He saw the pain in her eyes, but he continued anyway. "I need to send my sister a letter tellin' her I'm comin' home, and I need you to mail it for me."

She stared back at him. How could he leave? How could he just go back to Virginia and leave her here? What about their plans? She had shared her dream of working at the Brown Hotel with him, and he had encouraged her, supported her, never doubted she would make it. Eventually, he became a part of that dream. She could not pinpoint the exact moment it was decided, but she knew in her heart they were going to make something of themselves one day. Together. And now he was ready to just leave all of that behind? Leave *her* behind?

She shook her hands free from his grasp, dropped the clean rug in a cloud of dirt at her feet, and turned to hide her tears.

He could tell he was losing her. He took a deep breath, trying to remain calm. "Sally, you remember what I always say to you? Even if the whole world's against us, I love you, no matter what."

"Yes, of course I remember," she whispered.

"Well, I want you to come with me."

"To Virginia?" She felt dizzy.

"Picture it, just you and me and a new life, Sally. We can forget this place and start over."

"I don't know, Daniel." Her heart pounded, her stomach churned, and as she looked back into those dark brown eyes, a voice in her head told her to slow down.

"Look, it sounds crazy, but I know we can make it work. I wanna be with you, Doll, more than anything, you know that. But I can't stay here." He cupped her cheek in his hand and gently rubbed his thumb across her smooth skin. "You understand why, don't you?"

"Of course," she said, and it was the truth. She knew very well why he was running, but that didn't make it any easier.

"I need to send a letter to my sister to tell her I'm fixin' to come home. With you, I hope." When she didn't answer, he pressed on. "I need paper and a pencil, and then I need you to take the letter to the post office for me."

He saw her hesitation and then remembered the bundle of canvas waiting at his feet. "Look here, I brung ya somethin' real pretty."

He picked up the bundle, and Sally gasped when he opened it to reveal a beautiful white dress. Huge bursts of orange flowers, like blazing suns, were scattered across the flowing skirt.

He held the dress out to her, and she took it from him with shaking hands. She fingered the delicate lace framing the collar, the tiny white beads sewn among the skirt's floral design. "Daniel, where'd you get this?" Her voice was barely audible.

"I saw it and knew it was just made for you, Doll. And pretty soon, you'll have a whole closetful of fancy dresses like this. Once we get settled in Roanoke, you'll see. You ain't never gonna want for nothin' again." He tentatively brushed back a frizzy curl of hair that had fallen onto her cheek. "I'm gonna take care of you, Sally."

"Daniel," she said again, more forcefully this time, "where'd you get it?"

A small, white hot flame ignited somewhere deep inside him, and a flicker of annoyance flashed across his face. "What's it matter where it come from? I just wanted to get you somethin' nice, that's all."

She looked at him a moment longer, looked down at the dress hanging from her hands, and whispered, "Wait here." She was gone a moment before returning with a piece of paper and pencil. When he took them from her, she bent to move the rug back in front of the door. It was now covered in dust, which she half-heartedly brushed away with her hands. "Come back after sundown and hide your letter under this mat. I'll post it for you first thing tomorrow."

His face broke into a wide grin of relief as she stood to face him again. "I knew I could count on you, darlin'." He gave her a quick peck on the cheek, stuffed the paper and pencil in his shirt pocket, and hurried back down the alley.

Sally stepped inside, closed the door, and leaned against it, unsure if her weak knees would hold her up much longer. After a moment, she grabbed a paper grocery bag from under the sink and shoved the dress inside.

She walked back towards the door and caught a glimpse of her reflection in the ancient, oval mirror hanging on the wall. She took a deep breath and smoothed back the wisps of hair that had come loose, her hands shaking.

Before she could change her mind, she grabbed the grocery bag and made her way out the door. She heard a distant clap of thunder and peered up at the dark storm clouds gathering over Waverly as she hurriedly made her way down to the solid brick building on St. Elizabeth Street. She arrived at the station as the first fat drops of rain began falling.

She cleared her throat to announce her presence, but the young deputy at the front desk merely glanced up at her before turning back to his paperwork.

She cleared her throat again before saying, "I need to speak with Sheriff Conner, please."

The deputy looked at her in annoyance before muttering, "She's busy."

"I understand, sir, and I mean no disrespect, but I need to speak with her right away. It's 'bout the death of Missus Bower," she replied, her voice a little more forceful.

The deputy sighed. "You'll have to wait your turn."

Sally nodded. She turned to the row of chairs lining the hallway, chairs filled with white men and women, some fanning themselves with their hats or mopping their brows with handkerchiefs. Quiet voices murmured around her as she filed past. She tried not to notice how the elderly woman glaring at her clutched her handbag a little tighter as soon as Sally sat down next to her.

She was suddenly aware of some movement to her left and instinctively glanced at the front desk. A woman stood there, whispering to the deputy, who nodded in understanding. After a moment, the woman made her way back to her chair, a satisfied smirk on her face, and the young deputy called out to Sally. "You there! You're gonna need to wait outside."

"Excuse me, sir?" Sally asked.

"You heard me. Wait outside."

"I beg pardon, sir, but it's pourin' down rain out there, and there's an empty seat right here." She willed her voice to remain steady despite a dozen pairs of eyes watching her.

"I don't care if a twister done sprung up out there. You need to git," he answered, turning back to his paperwork.

Anger bubbled up inside her, anger at the injustice of it all, this injustice she was supposed to accept as the way things were. The same injustice that left her daddy miserable and drowning in whiskey at the kitchen table. The same injustice that Daniel faced every time someone watched him with suspicion in a store, every time he was falsely accused, every time the police showed up at his front door.

She stood, but instead of walking to the door, she made her way back to the front desk. The deputy's face hardened, and shocked whispers followed her down the hall.

Sally was well aware of what could happen if she spoke disrespectfully to a white man in this town, especially a police officer, but every minute that ticked by was another minute a killer prowled the streets in Waverly.

She raised her chin slightly and took a deep breath. "You're wastin' time here. I don't think you understand. I need to speak with Sheriff Conner right now." She heard disbelieving gasps from behind her.

The deputy raised up to his full height, his voice growing louder. "How dare you speak to me like that? Listen, I'm not sure who you think you are, girl, but I've already told you. Sheriff Conner is busy, and you'll have to wait. I ain't tellin' you again." He rested one hand gingerly on the pistol holstered at his side. "You best remember your place."

She licked her lips and met his gaze, praying her voice would not crack. "She'll want to see me, sir, I promise you. I have somethin' to give her."

The deputy snorted. "And what could the sheriff possibly want from an onery colored girl like you?" She heard tittering from the chairs behind her.

She reached into the bag and pulled out the orange and white dress, then tossed it on the counter between them. "This. It belonged to Missus Bower."

CHAPTER SIXTEEN - SARAH

June 24, 2006

"My name is Sarah Harper. You must be Mr. Sims."

The elderly man smiled as he slowly stood to shake my hand, shifting his fishing pole to his left palm. His wrinkled hand squeezed mine tightly as he answered, "That's me! Nice to meet you, Sarah Harper." He sat back down in his blue collapsible chair with a huff and added with a flip of his hand, "And you can call me Frank. I don't answer to that Mr. Sims stuff."

I liked him already.

I sat comfortably on a flattened tree stump and wondered where to start.

"Frank, thanks for agreeing to meet with me. I know this whole thing probably sounds crazy."

"Well, I gotta say, when Mark called and asked me to meet with you, I was kinda caught off guard. I haven't even thought about Daniel Porter in years. Matter of fact, I can't remember the last time anybody mentioned anything about him, or any other previous cases." He chuckled. "Yep, I reckon you could say retirement's been good to me."

"It sure has! I look forward to the day when I don't have to think about anything work-related."

"Ah, it'll be here soon enough. Hard for me to believe I'm as old as I am, but when I try to get out of bed in the morning, I'm reminded right quick."

I laughed as he turned back to the water. I shaded my eyes with my hand and peered out over the pond, silently berating myself again for leaving my sunglasses at home.

We sat in comfortable silence as I tried to think of how to begin. There were so many questions I wanted to ask, and yet I had no clue how to start.

Frank saved me the trouble when he cleared his throat. "So, Mark tells me you have some questions about the case, huh?"

"Yes, actually, I do. I don't want to keep you from your fishing, but I'm looking for some information. Mark said you didn't prosecute the Daniel Porter case, but I was still hoping you could offer some insight for me. The truth is, I think my grandfather may have witnessed the hanging, but he is absolutely refusing to talk about it, almost like he's hiding something."

"Is that right?" he asked, his curiosity piqued. "What's your grandfather's name?"

"James Graham."

"Hmmmm.... James Graham ... nope, I can't say that name is ringin' a bell," he said. "He may very well have been at the hangin', though. Seems everybody in Waverly came out to watch, matter of fact."

"It sure looked that way from the newspaper articles. Were you there that day, too?"

He smiled and shook his head. "We begged Mama to let us go, but she said she'd jerk a knot in our tails if we even thought about headin' downtown that day. Del snuck off to watch it anyway, though. I made him do my chores for a month to keep me from tellin' Mama, but now that I think about it, I prob'ly could've gotten at least two or three months of work outta him!" He laughed at the memory, and I found myself laughing right along with him.

"Well, my grandfather would've been nineteen or twenty at the time," I said, "so I'm pretty sure he didn't need to get permission from anybody to go."

He nodded. "True enough. So you reckon he was there, but now he don't wanna talk about it?"

"Yeah, I just can't figure it out."

"Well, most folks 'round here knew Mrs. Bower back then, or at least knew about her charity work and her family's money. She was a good, Christian woman. Maybe he grew up knowin' her and just don't want to think about the awful way she died."

"Could be." I said, deep in thought.

"Things in Waverly was different after that summer, that's for sure. It was a pretty open and shut case, so I've been told, but people was scared even after it was all over. Nobody could believe somethin' so awful could happen in little ol' Waverly, Kentucky." He shook his head. "Anyway, I don't reckon I know anything 'bout your Grandaddy. Sure wish I could help."

I nodded and pasted on a smile, trying to hide my disappointment.

"You know what I like best 'bout fishin'?" he asked.

I blinked and stared back at him.

He cranked the reel, brought the rod back over his shoulder, and recast with surprising strength. The line flew far out across the shimmering water before the weighted hook sank with a plop. He cranked the reel once or twice to tighten the slack. We both watched the plastic bobber dancing on the water's surface, the wind shifting it slightly to the right. "Sometimes, you spend hours and hours out here and don't catch a damn thing," he said. "Oh, now and then they might restock the ponds and you'll catch more fish than you can shake a stick at. But other days, I throw this line out over and over and end up with nothin' to show for it at the end of the day."

"Why in the world would that be your favorite thing about fishing?" I asked. "That's the thing I hate most about it! "

"Well, it's a lot like life, don't ya think?" He smiled. "You're lookin' for somethin', reachin' for somethin', you keep castin' your line out, and sometimes it pays off and you find what you wanted." He reeled the line in and recast, the line flying out further across the pond than before. "But sometimes, you get nothing. You gotta wait awhile and try again."

A painful memory came to me, a memory of staring at a balled up Kleenex clutched tightly in my fist, Steve beside the bed. He squeezed my other hand, but I barely felt his touch. I was too focused on trying to contain the painful scream that was clawing its way up my throat. The doctor stood at the foot of the bed, and every syllable he uttered left my insides feeling ripped and shredded and raw. Words like "genetic abnormality" seemed to echo in the small, sterile room, and I heard Steve sigh beside me when the doctor said, "... can try again in a few weeks." Try again in a few weeks? Was he serious? This wasn't like learning to ride a bike, where you fall off and climb right back on, ignoring the painful scrapes on your hands and skinned knees. No, these cuts were too deep. I turned to face the wall, the hospital gown riding up my thighs as I shifted on the mattress. Steve's hand slipped from mine, and I squeezed my eyes shut. Our lives had become a nightmare, a hell that we couldn't escape. The traumatic, horrifying events of the previous night left me broken, and I knew without a doubt there would be no recovery.

Frank's voice snapped me dizzily back to the present. "You know, I can read people pretty well, and I'm gettin' a feelin' that you've got somethin' else on your mind besides how your Grandaddy might've saw that boy hanged."

I shook my head to clear my thoughts and stuffed the memory back down, down, down where it belonged.

"Well, sure, I've had some stuff going on lately, but this little mystery is the one thing I should be able to figure out."

He watched me, waiting for me to continue. When I didn't, he looked back at the water. "Hmmm ... sounds like this thing with your Grandaddy is a way to take your mind off your troubles. Keep you from worryin' about other stuff in your world that ain't makin' any sense. Is that it?"

I slowly let out the breath I didn't know I had been holding. "Yeah, I guess so."

"So then, maybe what you need instead of talking to me is to talk to him? Sometimes the fish ain't bitin', but ya know, if you wait until the time is right, you'll usually get just what you need." He winked.

Minutes later I walked back to my car, my mind made up. Frank was right. Maybe I pushed too much at first, but I had avoided the subject since then - even avoided visiting Grandaddy James at all, to be honest. Maybe I could try again, get him to trust me and open up a little more about what he had seen - or whatever he was hiding.

CHAPTER SEVENTEEN - LILLIAN

June 9, 1936

"Sally, you did the right thing by coming to see me," Lillian said with a reassuring smile.

Sally sat in the chair across from her big wooden desk, nervously rubbing a small button on her handbag. Deputy Mitchell stood beside the door, both to assist with the questioning, and also to keep them from being interrupted.

When the girl didn't reply or move her gaze away from the bundle of fabric on the desk between them, Lillian sighed and glanced at the clock on the wall.

"Sally," she began again, "This may be difficult, but please understand, you're not in any trouble here. I just need you to answer my questions. How did you come across this dress?"

Sally swallowed and slowly raised her eyes. "Well, ma'am, it was given to me by someone a short while ago." She bit her lip. "He acted like he bought it. But I knew as soon as he showed it to me that it belonged to Mrs. Bower. I remember seein' her wear it last Sunday mornin' on her way to the church. Not many in town can afford a dress like that."

"I see," Lillian nodded. "And did you know Mrs. Bower?"

"No, ma'am. Well, everyone knows ... I mean, *knew* of Mrs. Bower." Sally cleared her throat.

Mitchell walked forward in a huff and snatched up the bundle of fabric. "Who gave you this dress?" The frightened girl visibly flinched as he waved the dress in front of her face. "We need you to tell us right now, girl. You're wasting our time."

Sally looked up at him and then turned back to Lillian, wide-eyed.

Lillian sighed. She was so thankful that Mitchell was there to guide and help her, but why did he have to be so impatient sometimes?

"Mitchell," she said carefully, "perhaps you could give us a few minutes alone?" She smiled sweetly up at him.

Mitchell looked at her in disbelief, his mouth open. He looked at Sally, then back at Lillian before nodding. He stepped into the hallway, closing the door gently behind him.

It was obvious to Lillian that Sally was confused and frightened, but also that she was trying to protect someone. As she watched the girl sitting across from her, Lillian thought of her own daughter, Mary, who was about the same age. She saw how easily a young girl could be duped and used by a devilish criminal, and the thought terrified her.

"Sally," Lillian said in a quiet voice. "A lot of people judge me. I know you understand what that's like. They don't think I can do this job. They don't take me seriously just because I'm a woman. But women can do powerful things, Sally. Women take care of things. We get things done. We manage households, raise babies, and make sure there's food on the table. We do whatever we have to in order to take care of those we love. And Sally, I love this town. It's my duty to protect Waverly, to protect the people here."

When Sally didn't respond, she added, "You're the only one who can help me, Sally. Please. Help me protect Waverly."

Sally looked down at her hands in her lap.

Before Lillian could speak again, she heard Sally's small, frightened whisper. "I can't be responsible. I can't be the reason he's hanged, ma'am." The girl's eyes filled with tears.

Lillian's heart pounded. "What do you mean, Sally? Who?"

Sally looked up at her, and suddenly, it was as though the floodgates had opened and her words, growing stronger with each syllable, rushed out. A torrent of breathless fear and desperation, almost palpable, washed over the room and everything in it. "He's a good man deep down, Mrs. Conner. It's not his fault that he's treated so poorly. Somebody had to've given that dress to him, that's all, maybe so's they wouldn't be caught with it. And now, he's scared. He knows the police will be after him because they're always after him, and he knows he'll be hanged if he's arrested, and maybe the real killer is threatenin' him to keep him quiet somehow..." She stopped and took a few deep breaths, her eyes shining with tears. "Mrs. Conner, I don't know what to do."

Lillian was so close. She just needed a name. And yet, Sally was a frightened rabbit, quick to bolt if startled. She must be careful.

"Sally, this man you speak of who gave you this dress. Please understand that he never has to find out you're the one who told us about him." The ticking clock on the wall seemed to be taunting her. Every minute that passed, the killer might be getting further and further away, or worse, planning his next attack.

"But even if he didn't find out, I would know, Mrs. Conner. I would know, and I couldn't live with myself." She pulled a thin, yellowed handkerchief from her purse and dabbed at her eyes.

Lillian decided to try a new tactic. "Sally, you say this man couldn't have taken Mrs. Bower's life himself, but you know he had to get that dress from somewhere. Maybe you're right, maybe someone else killed her and gave him the dress, or sold it to him. Either way, he can help us find the real killer. We need to talk to him so we can make sure the true murderer is caught and duly punished. I hate to think that whoever did this terrible deed is out there free and walking the streets of Waverly." Lillian glanced again at the infernal clock on the wall.

"I don't know, ma'am." Sally looked doubtful. "You sure you just want to talk to him?"

"Why, sure! We've got a whole mess of neighbors and acquaintances of Mrs. Bower that we're interviewing. He could help us, just like them. If he's as good a man as you say he is, don't you think he would want the killer caught?" Lillian willed her pounding heart to slow down as she saw Sally processing what she had said. The room was absolutely silent, and she wondered if Sally was holding her breath, too.

"Well, if you find the real killer, he wouldn't have to hide no more. We could finally leave town." She nodded her head thoughtfully, and then turned to look out the window. "We're going to Louisville, you know," she said dreamily. "We've got it all planned out. I'm going to get me a job at the Brown Hotel, and he's going to go back to work at the distillery. We're gonna rent a little apartment there, and I'm going to make me some pretty yellow curtains to hang in the windows. Yellow's my favorite color, and Daniel said I can decorate our place however I want."

Lillian dared not move a muscle as Sally paused and looked down. "Daniel?" she finally asked. "That's his name?"

Sally sighed.

"Yes, ma'am. Daniel Porter."

“All right then. Is there anything you could tell me to describe him? Anything at all?" Lillian asked, struggling to keep her voice calm and steady.

"Well, he's kinda short. He’s about the same height as me. He was arrested a couple of times last year when your husband was still the sheriff, but that was all a mistake. And he's pretty particular ‘bout his clothes. He always makes sure his shirts are white and clean, and he fusses with the collars a lot. I always tell him nobody cares about that as much as he does, but he won't listen. He says a man's appearance is--"

"Sally, do you know where he is right now?" Lillian interrupted, her pen flying across the notepad.

"No, but I can tell you he'll be coming to the tavern tonight. He asked me to help him with sendin’ a letter to his sister. He's gonna leave it under the mat by the back door so I can mail it for him."

Lillian's shaking fingers fumbled as she tore the sheet of paper with Sally’s description from her notebook. She hated to rush the girl out, but they had to find this Daniel Porter and talk to him before he left town. Or worse.

Sally took a last look at the dress on the desk as she stood to go. When she got to the door, she said, "Oh, I almost forgot to tell you this, ma’am. He always wears a ring on his right hand. A black band with a letter D carved into it."

CHAPTER EIGHTEEN - DANIEL

June 9, 1936

Dear sister,

I surely hope you and John can find it in your hearts to forgive. I swear, I was just tryin' to take care of you that night. You're all the family I got left in this world, Ruth. I reckon Kentucky ain't no place for me. I'm fixin' to go to Louisville and catch me a train to come on home where I belong. I will write again soon. I love you, dear sister.

Your baby brother

Daniel read the letter again. Satisfied, he folded the thin sheet of paper and tucked it inside the envelope, then slipped it into his shirt pocket. He stood and stretched, rolling his shoulders and flexing his fingers. His hands and forearms were still slightly sore, the muscles screaming in protest when he tried to move something heavy or make a fist.

He moved to the doorway and looked out over the water. The sun was setting, and the sky looked huge and orange. A fisherman sat in a little boat about a hundred yards up the river, floating peacefully near a grove of trees on the opposite bank. Daniel thought it a shame they were the only ones there to appreciate the view.

He would miss this river when he got back home, no doubt. He had always loved water, loved the way the light danced across the surface, loved the idea that it connected things that were far apart. This same water flowed for miles, carrying things away to a new land, a new start.

And yet, he reminded himself, Virginia had a beauty all its own. The sun setting over the mountains could be just as breathtaking. Soon, he would be back there. Back with his sister. Back where he belonged.

Daniel checked to make sure his shirt was tucked in evenly. He smoothed his hair down and carefully buttoned his collar up to the top, despite the heat of the late afternoon.

He stepped out of the shed, his heart beating faster as he left the safety of that sanctuary. He felt exposed and vulnerable,. He pulled his hat down lower on his head and began walking up 1st Street. He took a right on Walnut, a left on 4th, and made his way toward Tiegg's Tavern.

He half expected wanted posters with his face would be plastered all over town by now. He casually tipped his hat in greeting at a couple of ladies sitting on a porch, fanning themselves and having glasses of sweet tea. They smiled and waved in return, and his hammering heart slowed to a reasonable rhythm. Maybe he still had a little time.

He rubbed the small callous where his ring should be and wondered again how he could have been so stupid. He had gotten a wild urge to slip one of Mrs. Bower's rings on his finger that night, just to see how it fit. He had put his own ring down carefully on the white lace fabric that decorated the side table and placed the heavy gold band on his finger, sliding it past his knuckle. He remembered turning his hand, marveling at how the gold glittered in the moonlight, and wondering what Sally would think about such an expensive piece of jewelry.

At that exact moment, he had heard a noise from the old woman's bed, and all his carefully laid plans flew out the window.

He shook his head to chase away the memories from that night and raised his hat slightly, wiping the sweat from his brow. The heat was unbearable despite the sun having disappeared hours ago, and he was pleased to see the streets were nearly deserted.

When he got to the tavern, he looked down at the frayed rug laying on the ground by the back door. He glanced around one more time, lifted one corner of the mat, and slipped the envelope underneath. He crouched there a moment and stared at the door, wondering if he should knock. It wouldn't hurt to talk to Sally one more time, to make sure she understood how important this letter was and what might happen if he stayed in Waverly.

He stood and raised his hand to knock, hoping Sally would come quickly.

Behind him, a sudden rustling sound and the click of a pistol being readied left him frozen, his fist suspended in midair.

"We been lookin' for you, boy."

CHAPTER NINETEEN - SARAH

June 27, 2006

Grandaddy sat in the chair next to me whittling a small piece of wood, a pile of shavings at his feet. It seemed some of my best childhood memories were of watching his wrinkled hands methodically transform a block of ordinary wood into a beautifully detailed figurine. I used to think he was a magician, to be able to create something so beautiful out of something so plain and ordinary. A shelf in my dining room was cluttered with some of my favorite figures, mostly birds, he had carved over the years.

He paused to cover his mouth with an old handkerchief as another wracking cough gripped his body. "That cough sure sounds rough," I said. "Are you sure you don't need to go back to the doctor and get it checked out?"

He stuffed the handkerchief into the front pocket of his overalls and shook his head. "I been fightin' it for a few days now, but I reckon I'm on the mend. It'll take more 'n a cough to keep this ol' feller down." He winked at me, and I watched his wrinkled hands pick up where they left off, rhythmically transforming the wood into a small bird shape.

I leaned back in the chair and looked at the clouds drifting lazily above, breathing in the delicate scent of honeysuckle. My mind drifted back to a long ago spring night when Granny Patsy took me out to the barn and showed me the honeysuckle creeping along the walls. I had buried my face in the perfumed vines, inhaling deeply - and then came the best part of all. Granny Patsy showed me how to pull the leaves off the bottom of the bloom, gently removing the fine strings from the petals so I could lick the sweet drops of nectar from their ends.

“You’re awful quiet,” Grandaddy said, snapping me back to the present.

I glanced at him. "Well, I've been thinking about something. You know how you told me a little about the Daniel Porter case when I stopped by last week?"

If I had not been watching him so closely, I wouldn't have noticed how he hesitated for a split second, his hands pausing before continuing the long, smooth strokes.

"Mmmhmmm," he grunted. He rotated the piece of pine to the back and began shaping the bird's wings.

"Well, I've been doing some research. There's a lot of information out there about the case, but I was hoping you could tell me a little more about what you remember," I said.

He frowned. "Baby girl, that was ages ago, and your Grandaddy is an old man. I don't reckon I remember much 'bout it, to tell the truth." I watched him rotate the bird and nod to himself, satisfied that the wings looked even in size.

"Is that why you went to the library and looked in the archives?"

He glanced up, and his hand slipped. The piece of wood clattered to the floor below.

"How'd you know that?" he asked, slowly bending to retrieve the wooden figure.

"I saw your name in the log book."

He grunted and adjusted his grip. I watched as he used the knife's sharp point to begin the intricate work of the feathers.

"I looked it up just 'cause it's been so long and my memories seemed kinda fuzzy. But it was a waste of time. Them damn reporters wrote whatever they wanted. That boy's lawyers was just as bad. They was supposed to be helpin' him, but you'd never know it. Even the black folks in town turned their backs on him." He shook his head. "It was shameful."

"But if he really raped and killed that woman, I honestly can't blame them for turning on him," I said. "I mean, from what I've been reading, it was a horrific crime, and Mrs. Bower was apparently just a sweet old lady."

"Well, 'course." He spoke slowly. "I ain't sayin' that boy didn't deserve what he got. I'm just sayin' things ain't always what they seem to be."

"Yeah, but you've got a terrible crime, a confession, and then the killer was hanged. It seems pretty straightforward, even if it was a media circus."

"Seems that way," he nodded, "but you gotta figure that trial wasn't exactly fair, either. There coulda been a lot more to it than what them lawyers said, that's all I'm sayin.' There's always two sides to every story, and that boy sure never got to tell his."

He stopped flicking the knife over the smooth piece of pine and looked up at me. After a brief moment, he shook his head and turned back to his knife and the small bird in his hands.

"Ah well, that's enough 'bout that. No sense in stirrin' up stuff from way back. It's like your Granny always said, Baby Girl. Some things is just better left in the past."

CHAPTER TWENTY - LILLIAN

June 10, 1936

Lillian sat in the chair outside the judge's chambers, folding and unfolding her hands, trying unsuccessfully to calm her nerves. She could only hope Judge Riney would listen to reason. She had talked it over with Deputy Mitchell and some of the other officers, and she could see no way around it. Keeping Daniel Porter in Clay County was asking for trouble. The death threats had been bad enough. They had been arriving daily since the arrest. Some were on plain, yellowed paper, the handwriting rough, the poor spelling rendering them nearly indecipherable. Others were on flawless ecru stationery, written with great looping cursive by a steady hand.

But things had moved beyond mere anonymous threats delivered by the postal service. Now, Lillian's fears were being made real.

The door suddenly opened, causing her to flinch, and then Judge Riney welcomed her into his office.

"Thank you for agreeing to meet with me this afternoon," she said as she took a seat across from him.

"Of course, of course," he waved his hand. "No bother at all, Madam Sheriff. How are things? How are you and the children getting on?"

She smiled sadly. "We're managing as well as can be expected, Your Honor. I feel like I honestly haven't seen much of the children lately, with this Porter case keeping me so busy. Thank goodness Mary and Jack can help manage things and take care of the younger ones."

"I'm sure they've been a big help to you," he smiled. "Now, what can I do for you today?"

"Sir, I wanted to come speak to you in person because I have an urgent matter to discuss. As you know, we're holding Daniel Porter as a suspect in the Bower murder, and I feel like we need to move him out of Clay County as soon as possible."

Surprise registered on his face. "What makes you say that?"

"We can't keep him here. It's too dangerous, for him and for my officers."

"Well, now, I don't know, Sheriff," he frowned. "He's already wasted enough of your time and resources, don't you think? Transporting him all the way to Jefferson County is going to cost a lot more taxpayer dollars."

"I do see your point, your honor, but you need to understand I've got a young black man from out of town being held in my jail on suspicion of raping and killing a white woman." She saw him flinch when she said the word "raping." "We are still working our investigation, gathering evidence, and interviewing witnesses. I need every officer's full support to see this investigation through to the end. I simply don't have enough men to deal with preventing what may happen..."

He held up a beefy hand and stopped her mid-sentence. "Mrs. Conner, I know this murder investigation is not what you had in mind when you agreed to take over your late husband's position. Lord knows I'd have never asked it of you if I could have foreseen these events. But let me assure you, the suspect is in the safest place he could be right now."

Lillian swallowed and counted to ten in her head before answering, willing herself to stay calm. She had always known Judge Riney to be a man of reason. He had been supportive when she had taken over as sheriff. She thought he had always kept her best interest, and the best interests of the people of Waverly, in mind. She could not fathom why he was going to be stubborn on this point.

"Your Honor, with all due respect, I must disagree. Keeping him here isn't safe for him or my men. The prisoner has received numerous death threats since he has been in our custody, and last night, some cowards left a burning cross on the lawn in front of the jail. This situation is quickly getting out of hand."

Judge Riney frowned and shook his head, "Mrs. Conner, he's a colored boy that robbed, assaulted, and murdered a white woman. The public is angry. They want justice. How do you expect them to react?"

Lillian felt her cheeks grow pink as she answered forcefully, "He's a colored boy that deserves a fair trial, Your Honor, no matter what my opinion is, or anyone else's for that matter. Of course I want justice in this case, but not vigilante justice on the front lawn of my jail."

He folded his hands and rested his chin on top of them, staring down at the massive black oak desk separating them. She tried to ignore his patronizing smile.

"Mrs. Conner, honestly. What do you think may happen?"

"I would sincerely hope nothing at all happens, but this town is on edge right now, and I can't predict how people will react," she said.

He shook his head and began shuffling papers on his desk. "I'm sorry, but it just seems unnecessary by my account."

Lillian sat back in her chair, stunned by his indifference. "Unnecessary?"

"Look," he continued, "I know you may feel inadequately prepared for this kind of thing, but I can assure you that you will have the full support of the courts to see this through to the end."

She sat staring at him in shocked silence for a moment, her cheeks flushed. "Inadequately prepared? Sir, I hope you are not insinuating I am unfit for office or in any way trying to shirk my responsibilities."

"I meant no offense, Mrs. Conner," the judge said.

She bristled at his tone. "It's *Sheriff* Conner, sir."

He nodded, "Of course, of course. Sheriff Conner."

She sat a little taller. "Your Honor, I will admit I never imagined finding myself in this position, but I also would never presume to pass my duties on to someone else simply to ease my burden or my own conscience. You must understand I can not and will not knowingly put myself or my deputies in a position that may result in harm."

"Sheriff Conner, I apologize if I have offended you in any way," he said, flustered. "That was certainly never my intent. I'm just trying to do what's best for the citizens of Waverly. Surely you can understand my point. It's a simple matter of logistics, really. Transporting that boy to Louisville, only to bring him back to Waverly for the trial, is a blatant waste of taxpayer money."

"I think we both know the real danger here, Judge Riney, and it's not wasted funds. People are frightened, and they want justice. I know Daniel Porter's life may not amount to a hill of beans to you, or anyone else in Waverly for that matter, but I cannot risk a lynching on my watch."

Now it was Judge Riney who seemed offended. "A lynching? Madam, surely you're not suggesting the good people of Waverly would resort to mob violence such as that," he said.

Lillian looked him straight in the eyes. "Your Honor, last night I saw a cross burning just fifteen yards from my office window. You and I have no idea what the people of this town might resort to."

He stared at her before shaking his head. "Well, a burning cross is distasteful, certainly, but it's a far cry from a lynching," he replied, seemingly rattled.

"Is it? Sir, with all due respect, that's not a risk I'm willing to take." Lillian held his gaze.

Judge Riney leaned back in his chair and exhaled deeply. "You know, Sheriff, my wife taught me a thing or two over the past thirty-two years, and one lesson I learned early on is that there's no sense in arguing with a woman once her mind's been made."

Lillian exhaled in relief, content with the knowledge that Daniel Porter would soon be on his way to Jefferson County and things in Waverly would be on their way back to normal.

CHAPTER TWENTY-ONE - JAMES

June 28, 2006

He brought his shuffling steps to a halt on the smooth pathway and leaned heavily onto his cane. Each day, the paved walking path from the small parking lot to Patsy's grave seemed to have grown a little longer. He gripped the cane tightly with one hand, a bouquet of fresh hydrangeas clutched in the other, and tried to slow his breathing. His heart hammered in his chest. After a moment, still panting softly, he resumed his trek, trying not to think about the day when he wouldn't be able to make this journey, when even his trusty cane and a rest stop now and then wouldn't be enough to carry his tired body this far.

Most of Patsy's family was buried in Estill County, where she'd been born, but he couldn't stand the thought of her being so far away. He didn't like to drive much anymore, especially at night, but this cemetery was on the east end of Waverly. He could leave the farm and be there in seven minutes. He had timed it more than once.

He came to see her everyday, though his daughter frowned and complained that he couldn't see well enough to drive himself anymore. And sometimes, in his weakest moments, he thought she was probably right.

As he slowly passed the other stones, he wondered about the lives of these people who were long gone. Each stone represented a life - someone's mother, father, sister, brother. He thought of them as Patsy's neighbors now. He wondered if their loved ones still came to visit. He never saw anyone else when he came to see Patsy, but he also usually came mid-morning, when most people were at work or going on about their daily business.

He was glad to see the landscaping crew had been a little more careful this time. Patsy's gravestone was free of grass clippings, at least. Last week when they mowed, the entire stone ended up covered in tiny specks of green, too small and too numerous for him to pick off by hand. Patsy always kept a clean house, and he knew she would be fit to be tied if she saw how untidy her final resting place had become. He brushed the green bits of grass off as best he could, but his body, which first begun betraying him several years before, had once again not cooperated. His back was stiff and wouldn't allow him to bend very far, his hip and knee joints didn't seem to want to move the way he needed them to, and he grew light-headed and shaky when he bent down and reached to brush some of the largest grassy clumps from the lower part of the stone.

He called the office to complain about the mess, and now he nodded in satisfaction to see they had listened to his grievance and done something about it. It was terrible how people had no respect for the dead anymore, felt no shame at leaving their graves in such a mess. In fact, he hoped that damn landscape crew had been fired after his call. If they were left to it, before long the whole place would be headin' to hell in a handbasket, and there were plenty of other crews in town that could do a much better job.

He leaned his cane next to Patsy's stone and placed one hand on the top for balance. Then, he bent to remove the dried out hydrangeas from the vase and replace them with fresh blooms. The flowers' familiar fragrance filled his mind with memories. He stood and used his cane to gently move each stem in the narrow container, nudging them this way and that until the large clouds of blooms showed no gaps in between.

When he was finally satisfied with the arrangement, he glanced around to make sure no one was nearby. He was sure it might seem strange to others, but he talked to her, there in the cemetery. Sometimes, he shared stories about the weather, or what he had been doing that week, or how the family was. Talking to her out loud provided a way of somehow connecting with her, even if he never heard her sweet voice in reply.

"The weather is a little cooler today, Patsy. Weatherman says it may rain tomorrow, but don't you worry. I'll still come and tend to your flowers. It just may be a little later than normal, after the rain's passed through. 'Course, you know that weatherman doesn't know what the hell he's talkin' about anyway. He's wrong more than he's right."

He turned and looked out over the sea of gray and white stones covering the hill around him. Birds twittered from the branches of oak trees scattered throughout the perimeter of the cemetery. He could hear the occasional car driving by, but at least the road wasn't visible from where he stood. He was thankful Patsy had such a peaceful spot to rest. He wouldn't have wanted her to be right by the road, where every passerby could gawk at him, intruding on his private visits with her. These visits, and these conversations, were just between the two of them.

He knew there had been a time before he married Patsy, that he once lived life without her in it, at least for awhile. But he didn't like to think about that time. Thinking about the past could be so painful - almost as painful as thinking about how you've lost a future with someone. Knowing that from this day forward, they will no longer be there to share the everyday moments with you, both big and small. He still couldn't get used to not seeing her, not hearing her voice everyday.

He looked back at the gravestone, staring down at the letters carved into the dark gray granite. *Patsy Louise Graham. Aug. 1, 1919 - May 12, 2005. Wife and Mother.*

He wondered, as he often did, if she would have approved of the design he chose. It was simple, but Patsy never liked for people to make a fuss over her. The most important thing was that it had a vase so he could keep a steady supply of flowers near her all the time. She always loved her fresh flowers.

"Patsy, I don't know why, but some days are so much harder than others. This week, I've had more of them hard days than usual."

He wondered if he should tell her about the things he was forgetting, how his mind was fading like an old photograph, his memories jumbling together until he couldn't trust himself about what was real and what was not. How he struggled to hide his fear that his memories were becoming a hopelessly tangled knot inside his head, one that he would never be able to straighten out.

"Last week, I headed to town to get a roll of chicken wire to make a trellis for my tomato plants. I move so slow nowadays that it took me most of the mornin' to get ready and get there, and then that nice young feller at the hardware store loaded it up for me even though I told him I could do it myself. I know this body's old and worn out, but I can still manage a damn roll of chicken wire. I got back and unloaded the wire from the truck, but when I carried it around the corner of the house, I saw three trellises already leanin' against the barn. I set tomato plants out back in April, Patsy, and made trellises to go with 'em when I did it. How could I not remember that?"

He was ashamed to think of what his daughter would say if she knew he was forgetting things almost everyday now.

"That's not all, Patsy. Just yesterday, I got out of the shower and looked over to see the faucet in the sink turned on to full blast. It must have been running the whole time I was in the shower. I can just hear you fussin' at me for wastin' water like that," he chuckled, remembering how Patsy had always kept a tight fist when it came to money.

He paused, wondering if he should go on.

"I've been forgettin' other things, too, Patsy. Lots of things." He shook his head and an anguished, choked sound escaped from his throat.

"You know what? It sounds crazy, but sometimes, I feel like you're still with me, darlin', like you just stepped out back for a minute to water the flowers or sweep off the back porch, and you'll come back in directly, fussin' at me for leavin' my boots in the hall. I swear I can hear you hummin' the way you always did when you was cookin' or wipin' down the counters. I even find myself walkin' back into a room I just left 'cause I thought I could smell your perfume. Sometimes I wake up in the middle of the night and, honest to God, I don't know where you are, Patsy. It scares me somethin' awful. I walk through the house, lookin' room to room, but I can't find you anywhere, and I don't understand it. I sit on the porch and listen to the crickets and wait for you, thinkin' you'll come back. And then I remember after awhile, and I feel the pain of losin' you all over again." He paused and his voice faded to a whisper. "How could I forget somethin' like that, Patsy?

How could I forget 'bout them closin' the lid on that box and puttin' you in the ground?"

He waited a moment in the silence. Even the birds had stilled their chirping.

"I'm scared, Patsy. I don't feel like myself. My body feels old and worn out, but my mind is gettin' that way, too. I know if I told anyone 'bout the bad days, especially them really bad ones when I can't remember where you are or why you're not there with me, they'd try to put me in a home. Darlin', I know I'd die if they did, only 'cause I wouldn't be able to come here and visit you every mornin'. I've talked to you everyday for the past sixty-nine years. I can't stop now. It would kill me, sure as anything."

He was afraid to say more, as if voicing his fear about what was happening to his mind would make those fears somehow more real. And yet, as he stood staring down at the gray stone before him, words began tumbling out of their own accord.

"There's somethin' else, Patsy. Sarah showed up the other day and said she had to write a report about Daniel Porter for somethin' at school, and she wanted to know what I knew about it. I don't know why her teacher gave her a topic like that," he paused. "Well, maybe he didn't. To tell you the truth, Patsy, I can't quite recollect how it came up to begin with." He shook his head in frustration. "Anyway, that part don't matter. What does matter is that it's been on my mind more and more lately. I can remember bits and pieces of that summer, that night, like flashes on a movie screen, but I've kept it buried for so long, the memories feel faded, like they're covered with cobwebs, or I'm looking through a window that's gotten all fogged up. You always said some things is better left in the past, but now I have to wonder, did you really believe that, Patsy? Or is it just somethin' you said?" He smoothed one hand over the granite stone and tried to imagine Patsy's face, what she would say if she were standing before him.

"Would you still say that if I told you everything 'bout that night? Everything's so mixed up in my head, I'm not sure I can trust myself to tell the truth, even if I wanted to. And how could you believe me when I can't even believe myself?"

CHAPTER TWENTY-TWO - DANIEL

June 11, 1936

Daniel stared at the long, thin crack in the wall by the door. He traced its starting point all the way to the corner - a thin, almost unnoticeable gray string stretching across the plaster, from corner to doorway, as if someone took a pencil and drew a thin line from one point to the next.

"Boy, I'm going to ask you again." The older detective's voice sounded dangerously quiet. "What happened in Mrs. Bower's apartment that night?"

Daniel turned his eyes to meet the detective's gaze for a moment, and then went back to looking at the crack in the wall. His attorney cleared his throat and shifted slightly in the chair next to him.

Daniel wondered if either of the detectives in the room knew about the crack in the wall. Surely, with all the time they spent in this room interviewing suspects, they had noticed it. He wondered how long the crack had been there. Maybe the pressure built up over the years, slowly, the building settling, walls shifting, until a small crack finally appeared. Or maybe it happened all at once, a slight shift in the building's foundation causing a sudden break in the plaster. It was hard to tell from across the room. He wished he could have a closer look, but he knew the minute he tried to stand and move around, these detectives would pounce on him.

"Listen, boy, this ain't no trip for biscuits," the detective growled. "Tell us what happened in that room."

Daniel tried to remember the detective's name. Smith? Jones? It was a common name, he remembered, and Daniel thought it fit. He must be a common man, or at least an average detective. He'd probably worked in this same role for years, passed over for promotions time and again. Now, here he was, partnered with an officer young enough to be his son, questioning a suspect in a room with a huge crack across the wall.

The younger detective in the corner chair shifted his weight forward and stared hard, as if he could force Daniel to talk just by sheer willpower. Daniel noticed multiple wrinkles in the fabric running down both of the detective's pant legs like a complicated road map. He wondered why the man's wife had not taken the time to iron his pants and shirt more carefully. Maybe, like Daniel, he wasn't married and did his own ironing. Either way, Daniel could see no excuse for such a shoddy appearance.

The older detective was still waiting for an answer. Daniel looked at him and sighed. "I got nothin' to say to you," he said in a calm, quiet voice. "*Sir.*"

The detective slammed his hand down on the table in front of him, and the resulting pop sounded like a gunshot reverberating in the small room. "Damn it, I don't know what game you're playin' at here, but it's over!" Daniel noticed a vein bulging in the detective's neck and a small bubble of spit at the corner of his mouth. "You said the jewelry was in your room, but Sheriff Conner and the boys in Waverly turned that place upside down and didn't find nary a thing. Then, you said it was in a box under the porch at the Smiths' place. They searched there, too, but nothin'. They're still followin' up, but it's nowhere to be found. So either someone's holdin' it for you, or you're just stringin' us along. Either way, my patience is wearin' thin. You best start talkin', boy."

Boy.

Daniel's face hardened, and he clenched his fists. He was so sick and tired of white folks talkin' down to him. He looked straight into the detective's eyes with all the hatred he could muster, and his words spewed out like venom. "I got nothin' to say to you. *Sir.*"

His attorney cleared his throat and leaned forward, resting his elbows on the table. "Gentlemen, perhaps we should take a short break so I can speak privately with my client."

His cheeks flushed with anger, the detective stared back at the attorney and then at Daniel. He glanced briefly over at the younger detective in the corner and gave a slight nod. "Fine," he said in a low voice, "but I hope when we come back, you've decided to tell the truth. Next time, I might not be feelin' so nice."

The detectives' chairs screeched across the floor as they stood and turned to leave. Daniel watched them go, then turned to stare again at the crack in the wall when they slammed the heavy metal door. How many men, both guilty and innocent, sat in this chair and stared at that same crack along the wall? He had a sudden revelation that the wall was like his own life. It seemed solid from afar, and yet it was split. An irreparable fissure in his life appeared the night Mrs. Bower died. One tiny crevice. One defining moment that caused a permanent fault between who he was before, and what he had become. A simple patch job might temporarily cover things up, but the damage would always be there, lurking just below the surface.

He realized his attorney had been talking for several minutes, his voice soothing and quiet, but Daniel hadn't heard a word the man said. He noticed the attorney's cheap suit, the way the cuffs of his pants were ragged, threads popping out along the seams. He wondered how many black attorneys there were in Louisville and realized he could not recall this man's name. Beads of sweat lined the attorney's forehead, and he frowned as he shuffled his stack of papers back into his file. Daniel almost felt sorry for him and wondered how he got stuck with a case like this. White woman murdered, young black man from out of town who'd been in trouble before, and there you go. Open and shut. Isn't that what they called it?

The door opened and the detectives entered again. The older detective carried a small glass of water in his hand. He scraped the chair back and sat down heavily, placing the glass of water in front of Daniel.

"Are you ready to tell the truth?" His voice was calmer, though his eyes still blazed with anger. Daniel wondered if he had been in the hall right outside the door the whole time.

Daniel looked at the water glass sitting on the worn table between them. That table formed a barrier, a representation of all that had gone wrong in his world, all that had held him back. It was a dividing line, separating criminal from police. Black from white. There was no common ground, and there never would be. There was also no point in fighting anymore. He would always be on the wrong side of the table.

CHAPTER TWENTY-THREE - LILLIAN

June 11, 1936

"Be sure and check every little nook and cranny, gentlemen. It could be anywhere," Lillian reminded them as she glanced around the old barn. She stood just inside the doorway, unsure of what to do. Was she expected to comb through the area for evidence like the other officers, or, as the sheriff, was she supposed to supervise and only watch as the others searched? She tried to imagine what Everett would do in this position, but her mind was blank.

At least she knew what they were looking for this time. Searching the crime scene had been a nightmare. Her eyes had been drawn like a magnet to the body. All she could think was how horrified Mrs. Bower would be to have all of these men in her bedroom, poking through her personal things, while she lay there in bed with only a thin piece of fabric to cover herself. Lillian had felt a sudden, overwhelming urge to clear everyone from the room. Before she opened her mouth, a deputy pointed out a small marble bird figurine near the bed with what appeared to be blood coating its feathers. She stared at him wordlessly until he explained it may have been used as a weapon.

"Of course, of course," Lillian nodded in reply. Thank God for capable officers and observant men like Robert Clayton, the coroner, who noticed the black initial ring on the table by the door. In a daze, she had foolishly glanced right over it without a thought that it might be a piece of evidence.

She found herself snapped back to the present by a detective's voice calling, "Over here!" from across the barn. She hurried over, along with Mitchell and the others. Officer Thompkins was balancing precariously on an old trunk and holding up an old, rusted metal can. He shook it gently and then held it down for the others to peer inside. There, nestled among some small scraps of metal, Lillian saw a shimmer of gold and a collection of milky white pearls.

"Well done, Thompkins, well done!"

The officer beamed as she reached carefully to take the can from his hands. She turned to the others. "Now, keep searching, gentlemen. We can't afford to miss anything."

As the others moved off to continue the search, adrenaline now pumping through their veins, Deputy Marshall approached and offered to accompany Lillian back to the station to log the evidence.

Lillian breathed a sigh of relief when they stepped out of the barn. She was glad they had finally found something solid. Now, they could move on to the next step in the investigation. But what exactly *was* the next step?

As if reading her thoughts, Mitchell said, "So, the police in Jefferson County called and said Porter gave them a signed confession. Now, we've found the victim's personal belongings hidden in a barn near Porter's home. We'll continue taking statements and interviewing witnesses, but it seems like we've got our man."

"Yes, and I, for one, am very relieved," Lillian confessed. "It should be an easy case from here on out, don't you think? I mean, as easy as prosecuting a murder case can be, I suppose."

"I would think so," he answered slowly.

She looked at him and smiled, confusion registering on her face. "What?"

"Well, there's just a few things that don't quite add up," he glanced at her and then back down, as if voicing his concerns was the last thing he wanted to do.

"What do you mean, Mitchell? Is there something you're not telling me?"

"Oh, I don't know." He shrugged and shook his head, avoiding her gaze.

"Deputy, if you have doubts about this investigation, tell me right now. Please."

He hesitated only a moment before nodding. "I guess you ought to know. Well, when the sheriff's office called from Jefferson County, they said Daniel Porter confessed, right? And that's good, of course. But he also told them the jewelry was in three different places before we found it. We've established Mrs. Bower had quite a large collection of jewelry. What if there are other things missing?"

"Daniel Porter has told us story after story and sent us on wild goose chases all over for this jewelry. I doubt if he even remembers what he did with the rest of it. It could be in the barn or half a dozen other places he had connections to." She shook her head. "I'm sure the rest will turn up eventually, but we can't let that hinder our investigation. He confessed, and we've got enough evidence now to tie him to the crime."

He frowned. "Yes, I suppose so.'

"What now?" She couldn't hide the exasperation in her voice.

"Well, he also told the detectives he had an accomplice. I don't think we've spent enough time following up on that."

Lillian's eyes widened. "Mitchell, surely you don't actually believe that crazy story that someone helped him?"

"Well? What if they did?" He shrugged. "We don't even know for sure what all was taken from her room. What if there really was someone else? They could be halfway to Chicago by now with the rest of her jewelry! Porter has some sort of injury to his foot. I'm not entirely convinced he could have climbed up there to her window on his own to begin with."

"I can almost guarantee you we'll find the rest of her jewelry here in Waverly. And his supposed accomplice, this Allen McDaniel? Porter couldn't even tell us anything about him other than a name and that he lived in Waverly. He gave no actual address for the man, no place of employment, no identifying information whatsoever other than a name he probably made up on the spot. Even the physical description he gave us was vague - 'a white man with brown hair'? Why, that's half the population of Waverly!" she snorted.

"I know, I know, but don't you think it's strange that he came up with a name like that right away when we pressed him? I mean, I'm not saying Porter wasn't involved or that he's completely innocent, but what if there's more to the story? What if there really was somebody else?"

She shook her head. "Mitchell, do you know the real reason we can't find Allen McDaniel? It's because Allen McDaniel doesn't exist. Besides, why would a white man in Waverly agree to assist a colored boy with committing a robbery and murder? Not only that, Porter actually claims the whole thing was this Allen McDaniel's idea to start with. It's ridiculous!"

"I know, but it's like a gut feeling I just can't shake. Porter should know no one would buy a story like that in a million years. So why would he even tell it to begin with?"

"Why, Mitchell, you're 'bout as bad as that girl who gave us the dress. Next thing you know, you're going to tell me Daniel Porter is a good man, and that he's just been misunderstood!" She let out a harsh laugh before glancing at him and softening her tone. "Look, I'm not sure why he would say it, but don't forget he also admitted he'd been drinking at Tiegg's earlier that night. I don't mean to shoot down your theory, I really don't. You know I respect you, and you certainly have more experience than I do in this area. I just think we have to look at the most logical explanation here."

"I know. You're right. This Allen McDaniel thing just keeps nagging at me," Mitchell shrugged. "I can't help it."

"Well, if it makes you feel any better, we spent all day interviewing everyone with any connection at all to Daniel Porter, even went door to door in the colored section of town in case we missed something. No one has ever heard of Allen McDaniel. I'm telling you, it's another one of Porter's fantasies, that's all. Just one of his crazy stories."

"I guess so," he nodded, but she saw the doubt in his eyes.

She looked at him and for a moment, just a moment, she wavered. He seemed so sure, so convinced they could have missed something. Everett always respected and trusted Deputy Mitchell. She knew he was not one to make rash decisions without first weighing the evidence. And who was she? A woman with no criminal justice experience, no experience in law enforcement at all, and yet she was the sheriff. It was almost laughable. What if she really was overlooking something important, leading them down the wrong path?

She shook her head to clear the doubts from her mind. No. Everett would never have questioned Porter's guilt - not with a confession and evidence to tie him to the crime like this. There was no way she was going to let Daniel Porter throw them off track with another of his fanciful stories.

Mitchell stopped walking and turned to look at her. "Sheriff, I apologize. I don't mean to presume anything or make you to doubt your decisions in this case," he said.

"I don't doubt anything," she said, though she wasn't sure if she was trying to convince Mitchell or herself. "Daniel Porter is guilty, and he did this terrible thing all on his own."

"Yes, I suppose you're right," Mitchell conceded. He turned to continue walking down the sidewalk, and she followed, a step behind.

Lillian sighed with relief. "I'll be so glad to wash my hands of this whole thing. Once he's found guilty, he'll be sent to Eddyville to await execution, and we can move on. I, for one, will be thrilled if I never hear the name Daniel Porter again."

CHAPTER TWENTY-FOUR - SARAH

June 28, 2006

I scrambled and finally found my cell phone on the bedside table under a book and several balled up Kleenexes.

"Hey, Mama," I said, somewhat breathless.

"Hi, Sarah. I know you're getting ready for work, but I wanted to give you a quick call. We need to talk about something." Her sharp tone took me by surprise.

"Sure. Is everything okay? You sound upset." I racked my brain, trying to think what I could have done to upset her. Mamaand I had never had the closest relationship, but we rarely argued, and I couldn't think of a possible reason for her to call so early.

"No, Sarah, everything is definitely not okay. Can you tell me why you've been bothering your granddaddy about that boy that was hanged back in the 1930s? He says you keep asking him all kinds of questions, even though he told you he didn't want to talk about it."

"Mama, it's not like that," I said. "I haven't been bothering him. I had some questions. It's no big deal."

"No big deal? It sounds like a very big deal to me. He said you came by the house and practically interrogated him. How could you do that, Sarah?"

I sat on the edge of the bed, not quite sure how to respond. I felt betrayed. Betrayed that Grandaddy James had told her, and betrayed that she didn't understand. "Of course I haven't been interrogating him. It's just this thing I've been researching. I have to write a paper for one of my classes, and I had never heard anything about that execution. Did you know Grandaddy James was there and saw it?"

She cut me off, annoyed. "Well, of course I knew he was there. Everyone in Clay County was there. Listen, Sarah, he doesn't want to talk about it. He never has."

"What do you mean, 'he never has'? Have you asked him about it before?" I waited, holding my breath.

She was silent for a moment. "Look, he's never talked about it to me, and he sure isn't going to talk about it with you."

"But why? He was there when this execution happened. So what? You said yourself that all of Clay County was there, plus thousands of other people from all over the country. Why won't he talk about it?"

"I don't know, Sarah. There are things in your grandfather's past that he wants to keep in the past, and this is one of them."

"What kinds of things?"

"It doesn't matter," she said. I could hear the frustration in her voice. "Stop snooping around and let it go. I don't want him to feel anxious every time your car pulls in his driveway."

"I know, but I ..."

"Sarah, just drop it!"

I felt as if I'd been slapped. I sat clutching the phone, tears welling in my eyes.

Her tone softened. "Sarah, honey, I'm sorry, but I know how you get about things like this. I've told you for years that there's a difference between being curious and being obsessed. You never know when to let something go. Please try to remember, your grandfather is ninety years old. He's not been feeling well, and he doesn't need to go getting all worked up about stuff like this. Let him have some peace."

"I guess you're right," I muttered with a sigh.

"Thank you, honey. I'm sorry if I hurt your feelings. But I don't want you to upsetting him. I'm worried about him. He has an appointment with his heart doctor next week for a check up, so hopefully they'll let us know if there's anything serious going on with him. I think we need to try our best to keep him from getting all stressed out or worked up about anything," she said.

"Mama, it's fine, really," I said.

A few nights later, I sat curled up in my favorite chair, the phone pressed to my ear.

"You feeling okay?" Steve asked.

"Yeah, I'm fine. It's just been one heck of a week," I mumbled. "I finally got my research proposal submitted. I'm waiting to hear back from the professor now. I don't know what I was thinking, signing up for two grad classes this summer. With these summer sessions, it's like they try to cram a whole regular semester's worth of material into a few weeks." I sighed. "Thank God for Saturdays. Maybe I can get caught up on some things today."

"Yeah, well, Saturdays don't do much for me when I'm stuck at the airport," Steve replied in frustration. "I cannot believe they delayed this flight. This is what happens when I have a trip right before a holiday weekend. With all the delays and the flights all being overbooked to start with, it's been a nightmare."

"Um, did you check the weather? That storm system is huge. I want you home in one piece, even if it takes you a little longer to get here." I poured another cup of coffee and shuffled to the window to look out over the backyard. Ominous dark clouds loomed in the distance, and I wondered if they were connected to the same storm system that had Steve stuck in Ohio.

"I know, I know," he said. "So, what else has been going on? You said you submitted your research proposal. Have you made any more progress with your actual research?"

"Some. I stopped by to visit Grandaddy the other day after work, but he still wouldn't really tell me anything. It was so strange. I got the impression he was almost trying to defend Daniel Porter in some weird way, like he felt sorry for him or something. He mentioned how everyone was against him, and said even his lawyers and the black community didn't support him. But then, all of a sudden he shut down and wouldn't talk about it anymore. Then Mama got all mad at me."

"Wait, why was she mad?"

"Well, apparently, Grandaddy James called and told her I was snooping around and asking him questions, and she called me to basically yell at me and tell me to back off. She kept talking about how old he is, and how is health isn't the best, and we don't need to upset him."

"Whoa ... I'm sorry, honey," Steve said. "Are you two okay now?"

I sat at the kitchen table and looked at the piles of research scattered around - newspaper articles, my own handwritten notes, and a thick envelope from the Jefferson County Judicial Center's law library. "Yeah, I think so. It's fine. She probably does have a point. If he hasn't talked about it sometime over the past seventy years, he's not going to now. I mean, why would he?" I sighed. " I'm worried about him, too. He didn't sound very good when I was over there the other day."

"I'm sure he's fine. He's going to outlive us all, remember?"

I laughed. "Yeah, so he says. At least the trial transcript arrived yesterday, so maybe I'll get some more details from that. Mark was able to somehow pull some strings and have it sent by express mail. I guess he feels guilty about piling so much work on me to get things ready for this trial, so he decided to do me a favor."

"Well, maybe you can find what you're looking for in the transcript. Although, I think reading trial transcripts sounds even more boring than sitting in this airport all day trying to avoid making eye contact with total strangers."

I giggled. "Well, you'll be glad when I get some answers, trust me, if for no other reason than so you won't have to listen to me talk about it all the time."

Steve chuckled. "Mmmm, true story. I hadn't thought about that benefit." He suddenly grew serious. "So, you sure you've been feeling okay? How did your appointment with Dr. Alvey go?"

The air rushed out of the room.

"I cancelled it," I said in a flat voice.

"What? Sarah, why in the world would you cancel it?"

"I didn't feel like going, that's all." I waited, but all I heard was silence. "Steve, I'm just not ready, okay?"

"Are you sure? I mean, I thought we talked about this."

"I think mostly it was *you* talking. I just said we'd have to wait and see, and now I'm telling you I'm not ready."

"Okay, okay. Geez. I just thought we were on the same page about this, that's all. I mean, Dr. Alvey seemed to think we could try again in a couple of months, and it's been three now."

"Yes, I know. Listen, can we please talk about something else?" I asked, thankful he couldn't see the tears filling my eyes.

He sighed. "Okay. My phone battery's almost dead anyway, so I need to find a place to charge. I think I'm going to go get some coffee and find a quiet corner to read until they decide to fly this plane. They've already delayed us twice, but surely to goodness we'll be boarding in a couple of hours. You sure you're okay?"

"Yep, I'm fine," I wiped my eyes with the back of my hands and fought to make my voice sound chipper. "I'm gonna make some more tea and see what I can find in these transcripts. Keep me posted about your flight."

"Will do." He paused a moment, and I could imagine the look of concern on his face, the lines of worry I had seen there way too many times over the past three months. "I love you, Sarah."

"Love you, too."

I slowly stood and walked to the kitchen to put my empty mug in the sink. I glanced out the window at the clouds still brewing in the distance. The storm would be here soon.

CHAPTER TWENTY-FIVE - SALLY

June 13, 1936

"Sally, you feelin' alright?" Hershel asked with concern.

She realized she had been holding the same glass and wiping it absently with her towel for several minutes.

"What? Oh, I'm fine, Hershel," she said, setting the glass on the shelf and turning to wipe down the counter.

"You look plumb tuckered out, girl. Maybe you need to go take you a rest 'fore the dinner crowd gets here."

"Aw, no, sir, I'll be fine." She tried to muster up a smile of reassurance, but simply could not manage it.

"Are you sure? I can finish up here," he said, stepping closer. "Have you eaten anything today?"

She appreciated his concern, but she honestly could not remember if she'd eaten anything that day, or even the day before. Things like food didn't seem to matter anymore.

"Thank you for worryin' about me, truly, but I'll be alright. It's just this heat." She slowly shifted chairs around a table. Each chair felt as heavy as a huge boulder, but leaning against them at least kept her from falling to the floor.

"Lord, ain't that the truth?" Hershel answered, shaking his head. "Can't even step outside without comin' back in soppin' wet."

She nodded her head, too tired to reply. She shuffled over and grabbed a rag from the counter.

"Speakin' of heat," he said, "I better check and make sure we got plenty of ice, and you might want to slice up some more of that watermelon. I'm sure it'll go fast." He paused and looked at her. "I hate to keep askin', but you sure you're okay?"

She stopped wiping down the table by the window and looked up, smiling. In what she hoped was a convincing voice, she replied, "I'm fine, Hershel. Really. I've had trouble sleeping lately, and I've felt worn out like everyone else on account of this heat. Now, you go check on that ice and let me finish this up so I can slice some more of that watermelon, like you said. Marissa will be in directly, and I'll be needin' to help her get lunch ready."

Satisfied, he nodded and headed towards the kitchen.

Once he was gone, she stood and stared out the window, taking deep breaths and trying to calm her nerves. Since the arrest, she'd hardly slept a wink. She alternated between overwhelming guilt for going to talk to Sheriff Conner in the first place, and sheer terror that Hershel would find out about her relationship with Daniel and fire her. She needed this job. She closed her eyes and rubbed her forehead with the back of her hand, hoping her throbbing headache would subside. Oh, how she needed this job.

She tried to picture Daniel sitting in a jail cell, tried to imagine the pain he must feel at her betrayal. He had been right all along, of course. Sally was barely out of the sheriff's office before a group of deputies set out to capture Daniel. Now, he sat in a jail cell in Jefferson County facing the death penalty, and it was all her fault. A wave of nausea suddenly struck her, and she rushed out the back door, making it into the alley just before a torrent of vomit and bile came pouring out.

She stood gasping for breath, wiping her mouth with the back of her hand. She knew deep down that she couldn't help Daniel now, even if she wanted to. Her newest fear was what would happen at his trial. There was no way she could testify in court against him. She couldn't sit on a witness stand and tell the whole courtroom about the dress, and about how Daniel came to her for help. That was the real tragedy of the whole thing - all he wanted was her help. Instead, she betrayed him in the worst way.

Her blood ran cold as a terrifying new thought occurred to her. What if they tried to name her as an accomplice? Oh, she would not put it past that sheriff to make up vicious lies about her, to twist the truth and make it whatever she wanted it to be, to claim Sally and Daniel were some kind of black version of Bonnie and Clyde out to commit a crime spree and terrorize innocent white people. Meanwhile, the real killer was still out there somewhere, probably strolling the streets of Waverly without a care in the world, watching poor Daniel take the fall.

She couldn't understand how it had come to this. She only wanted to help. She only wanted to give Daniel a chance to tell his side of the story. How had things gone so terribly wrong? What would make Daniel confess to something he hadn't done? Did they threaten him? Beat him? She felt the guilt rising up in her again like a river threatening to spill over its banks. It might as well have been her own fists pounding a false confession out of him.

Another wave of nausea washed over her, and she bent to empty her stomach of what remained. She coughed and retched, her body contorting and heaving with each muscle spasm, turning itself inside out, but nothing else would come. She finally leaned back against the brick wall. She clenched her eyes shut and wished she could purge her anger and fear, could empty herself of the guilt until there was only a steaming puddle of mess in the alley. But it was a part of her now, taking root and growing deep inside her. No matter how hard she tried, she would never be rid of it.

CHAPTER TWENTY-SIX - LILLIAN

June 14, 1936

"Sheriff Conner, Mr. Allen will see you now." The secretary smiled cheerfully as she led her into the head prosecutor's large, well furnished office.

"Thank you," Lillian murmured as she stepped in and sat in a stiff leather chair across from an enormous, elaborately carved desk.

"Well, what have you got for me, Mrs. Conner?" Allen said, folding his large hands in his lap and leaning back in his chair.

"Mr. Allen, first off, I want to tell you how much I appreciate you seeing me. I know what a busy man you are."

"Of course, of course," he waved dismissively.

“Well, sir, we've been working almost 'round the clock. I think you'll be pleased with what my officers have assembled for you. It seems a pretty straightforward case. Deputy Mitchell will be delivering our files this afternoon, but I brought my notes and summary for you." She opened the folder and passed it to him across the desk.

She sat on the edge of her seat, unsure whether she should keep talking or remain silent until he finished flipping through the pages. She licked her lips and smoothed out her skirt while he read. She imagined Everett presenting case files in this very room, across the same desk. She was sure he had never felt this unprepared.

Finally, Mr. Allen closed the folder and looked up at her. "So what do you think, Mrs. Conner?"

"Well, sir, the victim was found in her bed, with bruising on her face, head, and neck. Doc Baker and Coroner Clayton both believe she was beaten and strangled, though the body was in such a state that they were unable to verify the exact cause and time of death. A marble bird statue, presumably used during the attack, was found near the bed. The sheets and blankets were pulled over her body, but when removed, officers noted the victim's gown had been pulled up above her waist."

She stopped, wondering whether to continue.

"And?" he prodded.

She took a deep breath and willed her voice to remain steady. She must not falter now. "According to the coroner's report, the physical evidence indicates she was assaulted before her death, and the attack was particularly vicious." She felt her face redden, her cheeks grow hot and flushed. She swallowed and stared straight ahead, sure Allen had been expecting this. Of course he knew she would struggle when explaining the more sensitive details of the case. He had been among the first to cry foul when she was appointed to take her husband's position to begin with, sure that a woman was incapable of performing the required duties of the office. She could not give him the satisfaction of seeing her falter now.

She cleared her throat and looked directly back at him. "It appears she was sexually assaulted," she continued. "There was a large amount of blood and internal tearing."

"I see," he nodded grimly. "Is that it? Any evidence to link Daniel Porter to the crime? Fingerprints, perhaps?" He stared at her, and she had the overwhelming sense that this was all for show. He had already talked to Robert Clayton and Doc Baker on his own; they had told her as much. Officer Stanton said Allen had called the station earlier that morning to inquire about fingerprints or other evidence found at the crime scene. She knew this was more about her than it was about the evidence, or even the case itself.

"There were no viable fingerprints found," she answered cooly. "They were either wiped clean, or perhaps compromised by the neighbors or those who arrived first on scene. We did find one print on the windowsill, but it was only a partial print and not a match to any we have on file, so it will not be submitted as evidence."

"Any witnesses?"

"No, sir. We do have a confession, although I'm not sure it will be admissible. We do have some items that belonged to the victim. Daniel Porter sent us searching for them all over the place, but we finally found them in a barn after questioning him several times."

"All right, let me make sure I have this straight. You found no fingerprints, no witnesses who saw Porter entering or leaving the scene, no real motive. You have a confession that may or may not hold water and a suspect who was not a close acquaintance of the victim." He frowned and shook his head. "Other than the fact that the suspect's third or fourth account of where some items were stowed away came to fruition, what actual evidence do you have for me, Mrs. Conner?"

Her heart thudded loudly, and she forced her breathing to remain steady. "His ring was found at the crime scene, sir. It was found in her bedroom, on a table near the body. Daniel Porter admitted it was his ring, and we have a witness who also said he was in possession of a dress belonging to Mrs. Bower. Porter gave the dress to her, in fact, and we have it in evidence now."

"Interesting. And this mystery woman will testify at trial as to the evidence implicating Mr. Porter?" he said, eyebrows raised.

Lillian hesitated. "Well, she's a very young girl, and she's understandably frightened by this entire situation. She's under the impression that Mr. Porter was involved, but insists he did not act alone."

"Would she repeat that while under oath?"

Lillian hesitated. "I'm not sure I'm following you."

Allen sighed audibly. "If she's convinced someone else was involved and says so while on the stand, it may introduce doubt in the jurors' minds and therefore prove detrimental to our case against Porter."

"Oh, I see." Lillian felt her cheeks flushing. Why hadn't she thought of that?

"Let's move on," he said. "Have you any other indication that he did in fact not act alone?"

"None that we can verify. He claims he was accompanied by an Allen McDaniel, and he says McDaniel is the one who assaulted and killed Mrs. Bower, but we've not been able to locate anyone by that name. Many of Porter's acquaintances in town are unwilling to speak with us, but those who have all indicate no such man exists. I feel this might simply be another of Porter's wild stories meant to distract us or keep us from learning the true facts of the case."

"I see." Allen shuffled through the papers on his desk. "Well then, I suppose the only matter to decide now is whether to charge him with rape or first degree murder."

Lillian sat back in her chair, her confusion palpable. "I beg your pardon, sir? Surely, he will be charged with murder?"

"Not necessarily. Murder may be considered the more serious of the two crimes, but I will need to investigate further. I should warn you, things could become quite complicated for you."

"How so?" she asked, hoping she didn't appear as ignorant as she felt.

"Well, Mrs. Conner, the state of Kentucky says if I charge him with first degree murder and he is found guilty, he will be electrocuted at the state penitentiary in Eddyville. If, however, he is found guilty of rape, the jury can sentence him to be publicly hanged in the county in which the offense occurred."

Lillian suddenly felt as if the room was closing in around her.

"That means," he looked directly at her, "that you, madam, would be required to oversee his execution."

CHAPTER TWENTY-SEVEN - SARAH

July 3, 2006

"Well, I'd say things went fairly well today." Mark loosened his tie as he put his briefcase on the chair by his desk. "We finished closing arguments this afternoon, so it's out of my hands now."

"That's great!" I followed him into his office. I felt truly happy for him. I knew how hard we had both worked preparing for this case.

"Yeah, at this point, I'm just ready for it to be over. Hopefully they'll call this afternoon. With tomorrow being a holiday, this thing could drag out for awhile longer." He sighed, running his hand through his hair.

"You just want this over with so you can get on that plane next week and head to Riviera Maya with no regrets," I teased.

"Amen to that. I can already feel the sand between my toes. I wonder if I could start a bonfire on the beach and burn all of the motions I've had to file with this one?" he asked as he reached into the small fridge hidden in the cabinet and grabbed a bottle of water.

I laughed before answering, "I'm pretty sure they have rules against that at your resort."

"True, true. Oh well. You guys planning to watch the fireworks show downtown tomorrow night? Looks like the rain might actually hold off this year."

"Yeah, we'll probably go. Steve's like a little kid when it comes to fireworks."

"I am, too. Trisha always laughs at me, but I can't help it. There's just something about watching explosions in the sky that gets me every time."

"Yeah, Steve gets way too excited about pyrotechnics. I don't get it. Maybe it's a guy thing?" I shrugged with a smile.

"Maybe so. Hey, I keep meaning to ask you. How are things going with that trial you've been researching?" He plopped into his desk chair and took a long swig of water.

"Well, I finished going over the transcripts last night. Parts of it were hard to read, knowing it was all true and not some crime novel. The prosecution sure didn't hold anything back when describing her injuries. I can't imagine family members in the courtroom hearing the details of what happened to her." I shuddered.

"Yeah, it's never easy with a crime like that. They had to make sure they presented a solid case. Plus, nowadays the judge is in charge of sentencing when a defendant enters a guilty plea, but back then in a capital case, it was standard procedure for the jury to decide the sentence. I mean, think about it. Hearing all those grisly details would make it much harder for the jury to let him walk or to give him anything less than the maximum penalty."

"That makes sense. I just find it strange that the prosecution called a whole string of witnesses, but the defense didn't call any. I mean, it's like they didn't try to build any sympathy with the jury, didn't give an alibi, didn't cross-examine half of the witnesses, didn't question the validity of his confession. I know they probably felt like they were fighting a losing battle, but it's like they gave up before they even started."

"Well, you have to remember this was, what, 1936? And they were trying to defend a black man accused of raping and murdering a sweet old white lady. A black man who, by the way, was known to be a liar and a common criminal."

"Okay, okay, you have a point. I can't help but think they missed some opportunities, that's all."

"Hey, what about your grandfather? Any idea yet how he was involved in this whole mess?"

"No, and that's a whole other problem. Apparently, he complained to Mama that I've been bothering him and trying to dig up things about the past. She basically let me have it and told me to back off." I rolled my eyes.

"Yikes," Mark said.

"Yeah, yikes is right."

"Anyway, thanks again for getting me the transcript. I think I'm going to try and read it again tonight before Steve gets home. Who knows, maybe I'll find something I didn't see before." I turned to go.

"Oh, wait ... there was one more thing I read that was pretty wild. He could have had several charges brought against him, really - rape, murder, burglary. Murder and rape were both capital offenses at the time, but one of the newspaper articles mentioned that the punishments were different. Those who received the death penalty for murder were electrocuted at the state penitentiary in Eddyville. If you were convicted of rape, a jury could sentence you to 10 or 20 years in prison, or they could sentence you to be hanged in the county where the offense occurred."

"And I'm guessing it's a safe bet that the publicity against him and the viciousness of the attack mean he was pretty much guaranteed the maximum penalty either way," Mark said.

"Exactly. The prosecution had to decide whether to charge him with murder and electrocute him in Eddyville, or charge him with rape and hang him in Waverly. I just can't understand why they chose hanging in Waverly, especially since it turned into such a fiasco."

Mark shrugged. "Well, I think it's pretty simple, really. Somebody wanted to see him hang, and they wanted Sheriff Conner to be the one to do it."

PART 3

THE TRIAL

CHAPTER TWENTY-EIGHT - DANIEL

June 24, 1936

There were fourteen panels of wood on the wall behind the judge. Daniel had counted them many times over the past several hours. He also noted the number of jurors wearing neckties (six) and the number of notebooks full of scrawling words spread across the defense table (three, which was two less than on the prosecution's table). He counted things over and over, looked for patterns, watched the second hand of the clock move around and around, and observed a fly flittering around the defense table. Anything to take his mind off of the proceedings, to block out the accusations being thrown around by the prosecution, to distract him from the eyes of the white men sitting in the jury box. Those men would soon decide his guilt or innocence, and more importantly, his life or death.

His attorneys (there were two) had told him during their pretrial meetings that they were there to support him, they were ready to help him gain his freedom, they would do all they could for him. Foolishly, he had believed them.

And so, he sat quietly, like they told him to, not saying a word. When the prosecutor began speaking in a soft tone about kind Mrs. Bower, telling of her generous charity work and selfless service to the community of Waverly, Daniel counted the thin spindles in the wooden railing that separated the jury box from the rest of the courtroom (twenty-eight).

He stayed quiet even when the victim's neighbor, Mr. Smith, described finding the body and running to fetch Doc Baker and Robert Clayton from the church at the corner of 4th Street. Daniel stifled a wild urge to laugh as he imagined a somber church service full of wide-eyed white people, Mr. Smith rushing down the aisle to whisper to Doc Baker and Coroner Clayton, the two men jumping up and following him out.

Daniel was silent when Doc Baker strode to the front of the courtroom and put his hand on the huge black Bible and swore to tell the truth, the whole truth, and nothing but the truth. A murmur of excitement traveled through the crowd like a flood among the rows of wooden chairs. This is what they came for - to hear the grisly details, to see if the rumors were true. Had she really been raped? Was the beating so severe she was unrecognizable? Did she fight back?

The good doctor spoke in a solemn voice about the blood on the sheets, the bruising on the victim's face and head, her swollen eyes, the scarf stuffed in her mouth to keep her from crying out. The doctor's voice echoed across the otherwise silent courtroom, the sound reverberating off the back wall and coming back again.

Daniel heard sniffling behind him and imagined Mrs. Bower's family hearing these details for the first time. He wanted to turn around, to look at their faces, but his attorney saw him shifting to look over his shoulder, frowned and shook his head. It was a quick, barely noticeable motion, but the message was clear. Be still. Stay quiet.

And so, instead of turning to look at Mrs. Bower's family, Daniel stared at the table before him and counted the small dents, scratches, and nicked places in the polished wood (eighteen that he could see, although there could be many more hidden beneath his attorney's papers, which covered much of the table's surface). He counted imperfections in the wood and tried to block out Doc Baker's voice as it went on and on, describing how he carefully removed a blanket from the victim's body and discovered her gown had been pulled up above her waist. Daniel heard a low moan and hushed whispers from the crowd behind him as Doc Baker described the sexual assault.

The coroner testified next, and Daniel clenched and unclenched his jaw as the man explained how the victim had at one point been rendered unconscious, either by asphyxiation due to strangulation or blunt force trauma, though he could not determine if this had occurred before or after the rape.

The prosecutor pointed his finger like an impassioned preacher, shouting that Daniel deserved "the maximum penalty for this most heinous of crimes!" Meanwhile, Daniel sat with his head down, counting notebooks and wooden panels and neckties and buttons on the prosecutor's shirt (six) and whatever else he could count just to fill his head with numbers and block out the words flying like bullets across the room. He glanced down at his hands gripping the arms of his chair so tightly his fingers ached, willing himself to stay in his seat and to hold back the angry noises threatening to burst out of his own mouth.

His head snapped up when the prosecutor's booming voice called twelve year old Raymond Rutherford to the stand. Raymond shuffled slowly forward from the crowd, pulling at his shirt collar and hiking up his pants that were at least two sizes too big. When he was asked if he swore to tell the truth, the whole truth and nothing but the truth, his "Yessir" was so feeble the court officer had to ask him to speak up.

After asking a few simple questions to put the boy at ease, the prosecutor hitched up his belt over his wide girth and was ready to get down to business.

"Raymond, when is the last time you saw Daniel Porter before today?"

Raymond scratched at a scab on his upper arm before answering, "Well, I saw him the Saturday it happened over by Daman Bryant's grocery store."

The prosecutor smiled and nodded encouragingly. "You mean the day Mrs. Bower was murdered?"

"Yeah," the boy said. A woman in the audience cleared her throat, and Raymond's eyes snapped her way. "Oh, I mean, yessir," he added quickly.

The prosecutor looked at the jury and chuckled before turning back to Raymond. "That's fine, son, that's fine. Do you know if the victim, Mrs. Bower lived near there?"

"Oh yes, everybody knows that. Old lady … I mean Mrs. Bower was always sittin' out on the porch just a few doors down from the store. I used to see her there all the time."

"I see. And please tell the jury, Raymond, about what time did you see Daniel Porter over there by the store on this particular day?"

"Oh, I reckon it was 'bout five o'clock," the boy said, concentrating hard. "I was on my way home from playin' baseball in the lot down by the courthouse. I had to be home 'fore dark 'cause Mama gets fit to be tied if I'm not home in time to gather the eggs before supper."

The prosecutor smiled. "Well, you're a smart young man, Raymond, for makin' sure you got home in time for your chores. Now, I just want to make sure. Are you positive it was Daniel Porter you saw that evenin' over by the store? Think hard, now."

"Oh, yessir! I know it was him. I even talked with him. He was limpin' pretty bad. Matter of fact, I asked him why he was walking like that, and he told me he had dropped an iron on his foot. Musta hurt somethin' awful. His shoe was all tore up because he said it hurt too much when he laced it like normal, so's he had to cut a hole plumb through it."

Daniel noticed the prosecutor's smug grin had disappeared.

No one said a word.

Daniel looked from his attorneys to the prosecutor and back again. He could hear his heart drumming loudly in his chest and wondered that the entire courtroom couldn't hear it as well.

Finally, the prosecutor turned to the judge, hitched his belt, and said, "Nothing further, your Honor."

Daniel held his breath and waited. Any minute now, his attorney was going to cross-examine this boy, plant doubts in the jury's mind. Obviously, the prosecutor hasn't expected Raymond to mention Daniel's foot. Otherwise, why would he have ended his line of questioning so quickly? Now was their chance. If they could convince the jury that Daniel's injury would have kept him from climbing into and out of the room on the second floor, they just might have a chance at establishing reasonable doubt.

The minutes crawled by. The head prosecutor lumbered over to his table and took his seat. He took a handkerchief out and wiped the sweat from his brow while Raymond Rutherford sat in the witness stand, unsure of what to do.

Daniel licked his lips and waited, quiet and still like he was supposed to. In fact, he was still sitting in silence when his attorneys said no, they would not need to cross-examine the witness, and no, they did not have any witnesses to call for the defense, and no, nothing further, thank you, Your Honor.

Daniel's breath rushed out so quickly, it ruffled the papers on the table before him. Raymond made his way quickly back to his seat while Daniel looked around wildly at his so-called defense team. He wanted to yell, wanted to scream at them, to ask why they weren't helping him like they said, to ask whose side they were on. But deep down, he already knew the truth. They couldn't help him if they wanted to. He had always known how this would go. Whatever doubt he might have had about his fate was erased the moment the white officers (two) had walked him into the courtroom packed with white faces, the white judge watching from on high, the white jury members (twelve) filing somberly into their seats. He had looked at the white attorneys sitting at the prosecution table (three), and he thought to himself that he had never been in a room with this many white people before. And once again, he was on the wrong side of the table.

CHAPTER TWENTY-NINE - LILLIAN

June 25, 1936

She sat staring straight ahead, hands folded neatly in her lap. She could feel knots of tension in her shoulders, the result of hours of sitting and staring ahead like this. She had steeled herself for this day, the day of closing arguments at the end of what felt like a long and arduous trial, though it had actually lasted less than a week.

Lillian had thankfully not been called to testify, no doubt due to the prosecution's unwillingness to distract from the viciousness of the crime. A female sheriff's testimony could be quite the novelty and might cause jury members to lose focus. Instead, she had watched as a parade of her officers and deputies presented their testimony before the packed courtroom. They described the first panicked moments when they found the crime scene in disarray, the careful process of collecting evidence, and finally the hunt for and capture of Daniel Porter.

As she listened to their words, she felt honored to call them her colleagues, especially Deputy Mitchell. She could see he was a bundle of nervous energy, his leg bouncing up and down as he crossed and uncrossed his hands in his lap while on the stand. And yet, he presented the facts and answered the prosecutor's questions thoughtfully and clearly, the jury members hanging on every word. She knew Everett would have been so proud of him, as she herself was.

She glanced over at Daniel Porter. He wore a crisp, freshly pressed white shirt and sat stiffly in his chair, his back rigid. She had been watching him, but he had not turned to look at the jury, had hardly acknowledged his attorneys. The courtroom's low murmuring became instantly silent as every ear strained to hear him speak when the judge asked if he planned to testify on this own behalf. He uttered the words, "No, sir," and she was surprised at the softness of his voice, just as she had been surprised at his small frame when she first laid eyes on him the night Deputy Mitchell and Officer Johnston brought him into the station. He simply did not look like a killer. She guessed his weight at no more than 130 pounds, his height a little over five feet. In fact, she realized with a start, he was about the same size as her son, Jack.

The lead defense attorney stood and informed the judge the defense had no closing argument. The judge nodded and turned to address the members of the jury. She watched the jury closely as the judge gave his final instructions. She tried to imagine herself in their position, about to decide the fate of the young man sitting a few yards away. She knew from Mr. Allen that the jury consisted mostly of farmers along with a couple of shopkeepers. All white men, of course.

They stood and filed silently out of the courtroom. The clock on the wall read 12:18. The crowd began a quiet murmuring, no doubt speculating on how long it would take the jury to reach a decision and where to grab a quick lunch before heading back. Those lucky enough to have seats were reluctant to give them up, but there was no telling when the jury would return.

Lillian wiped her brow with her handkerchief and thought again of Sally. She had failed her, failed on so many levels. She had pushed too hard, her desperation to find the killer overriding her judgment, causing her to make promises she knew she couldn't keep. Mitchell had assured her she had done the right thing, and yet she was tormented by thoughts of what might happen to the young girl, so trusting and so naive. Sally was just a girl who got tangled up with a dangerous man and had done what she thought was right, only to be betrayed by the very people she thought could help her. Perhaps no amount of reasoning would have gotten through to Sally and convinced her of Porter's guilt, but Lillian still wished things had turned out differently.

Porter's attorneys leaned over to speak with him at the defense table, one on either side. Lillian marveled at how Daniel still stared straight ahead, not seeming to register that they were even speaking to him. The prosecution had quickly began packing their briefcases when the jury left the courtroom, but the defense seemed reluctant to go, as if resigned to the fate of their client, but unwilling to say goodbye. He looked so small between them, almost like a child.

Lillian licked her lips and tasted the salt of sweat. The courtroom was stifling, even with the paper fans in virtually every observer's hands, striving in vain to move the stale, hot air around. The putrid smell of body odor permeated the crowd. She looked toward the massive double doors behind her and considered stepping out for some air, but then remembered the throng of reporters waiting on the steps outside. They would all be clamoring to get a picture or a statement from the female sheriff from Waverly who had handled the crime investigation.

She glanced again at the clock. 12:22. She saw that Daniel's attorneys were standing next to him at the defense table, the bailiff preparing to take him back to his cell. She had resigned herself to the idea of fighting the crowd and making her way out of the courtroom when a side door suddenly flew open.

A shocked murmur traveled through the crowd, a wave starting in the gallery above and traveling down each row, back to front, and left to right until it grew into a frantic rumbling. The jury members came through the door one by one and walked back to take their seats in the jury box. Lillian watched, confused, along with most of the others in the crowd. Why were they back already? Was there some misunderstanding about the sentencing options, or about the testimony or evidence? Was there some procedural step that had been overlooked? Her stomach dropped as she realized that a mistrial would mean going through this entire process all over again.

The judge entered the courtroom, solemnly striking his gavel to quiet the buzzing crowd. When he was satisfied, he turned to address the jury. "Ladies and gentlemen of the jury, have you reached a verdict?" His booming voice echoed off the walls, and the crowd held its collective breath. Lillian sat quietly, twisting her handkerchief in her hands. She looked down at it, remembering Sally, frightened and torn, doing the same thing in her office mere weeks earlier.

The foreman stood, gripping a piece of paper in one hand. "Yes, we have, your Honor. We, the jury, find the defendant, Daniel Porter, guilty of rape as charged in the indictment and fix his punishment at death by public hanging in Clay County, where the offense occurred."

Everything seemed to happen at once, a single moment and one statement transforming the courtroom from a quiet, orderly proceeding to a tumultuous, deafening storm. The judge banged his gavel, demanding order in the court, but the sound barely registered among the ecstatic throngs. Reporters rushed out to file their stories, Mrs. Bower's family embraced one another, tears streaming, loudly thanking God and the jury members, the defense attorneys spoke frantically to one another as a bailiff hurried to remove Daniel Porter from their midst, and the desperate judge ordered the courtroom cleared of the whooping and shouting onlookers. But in the eye of the storm, in the midst of this chaos, sat one woman. A mother. A widow, like Mrs. Bower. She sat alone among the crowd, alone with her thoughts and a twisted handkerchief in her hands, the enormity of the jury foreman's words crushing her like a boulder.

CHAPTER THIRTY - DANIEL

June 25, 1936

Someone grabbed his arm, perhaps a bailiff, and escorted him quickly out of the room, past excited newspapermen shouting questions and the judge banging his gavel.

He could still hear the judge's angry shouts as they walked down the hall.

He counted each door they passed (four) and realized that truth was only what people collectively choose to believe. In the end, it didn't matter how many people were in Mrs. Bower's bedroom the night she had been murdered (three).

CHAPTER THIRTY-ONE - LILLIAN

July 15, 1936

She paced the floor, wringing her hands. She felt so full of nervous energy that sitting still was impossible at the moment.

"I just can't be at peace with it, Father. I've turned it every which way in my mind, but there's no easy answer. I want to do right by the people of Waverly, and I would hate to make them doubt Judge Riney's decision to appoint me to this office."

"Lillian, no one doubts Judge Riney's decision or your abilities," Father Stuart answered. He offered her a smile and silently prayed that God would give him the words to say to comfort this poor child.

"Yes, but performing this duty as a sheriff is one thing. As a mother... well, now, that's a different story altogether, isn't it? And yet, they are two halves of me. I cannot separate myself."

She stopped in front of the window and stared out at the rectory's small garden below, desperately wishing for a way out. She was reminded of Jesus in the garden of Gethsemane, and felt herself echo His prayer in her heart. *Father, if it be Your will, let this cup pass from me.*

She turned and looked back at the elderly priest, who sat across from her with his hands folded in his lap. "Father, what will people think of me? And what about my children? I don't want them to grow up with the burden of knowing their mother was responsible for taking another person's life, no matter the circumstances. I don't want that to be what I am remembered for, what my children are known for."

She thought of her oldest, eighteen year old Mary, on the verge of venturing out on her own. Her middle two, Jack and Patrick, both enthralled by the publicity surrounding the case and not grasping its consequences. And her youngest, eight year old James. He seemed to struggle more than the other children when Everett died. Perhaps he saw how he was being forced to grow up too quickly. He was the youngest, but also the only of her four children who would grow up without his mother at home during the day. Instead, she was spending more and more time at the station, at a point when her children were still adjusting to the loss of their father and needed her more than ever.

Father Stuart waited for her to continue, and she marveled at his patience. How easy he made it appear to just sit and listen, and yet she knew how difficult it could be. How many times had she half-listened to what Everett was saying, instead eagerly awaiting her chance to jump in the conversation and share her own thoughts? What she wouldn't give now for a chance to sit and listen to her husband's smooth, warm voice again. She knew she would hang on every word if given the chance.

Finally, Father Stuart leaned forward and spoke. "Lillian, the Lord looks favorably on those who work hard. You are doing your duty in the role entrusted to you. The Lord hates sin, and those who break the laws of this world should be punished. Daniel Porter broke one of God's Holy commandments when he committed murder and took the life of an innocent woman. Be at peace knowing that, difficult though this task may be, you are not going up against the Will of God. You are in fact carrying out your sworn duty, as is fitting for your position."

She nodded her head and let out the breath she did not realize she had been holding. She was deeply thankful for this man who had been a confidant and advisor for her family for so many years. She remembered how he counseled her after Everett's death, during those dark days when just getting out of bed and getting food on the table seemed impossible. She wasn't sure how she would have made it without his shoulder to lean on.

"Lillian, I'm worried about you. You are under an enormous amount of stress, as anyone in your position would be. Add to that the burden of providing a stable home for your children after the loss of their father in the midst of these chaotic events. I'm afraid it's too much for any one person to bear alone," he said gently.

Lillian wiped her eyes before nodding, not trusting herself to speak.

"Perhaps I have a solution," he said with a gentle smile.

Twenty minutes later as she opened the door of her office, she felt a thin, tenuous thread of calm that she had not felt before. She respected Father Stuart, and the fact that he assured her she was doing the right thing by both man's law and God's law gave her the small boost of confidence she needed. The solution he offered for helping navigate this chaotic period in her life while still providing a stable environment for her children had been a relief, though she knew it would also be one of the most difficult undertakings of her life.

She sat heavily in the chair and noticed a stack of mail waiting on the desk. The jail had been flooded with letters from all over, each day's bag seemingly stuffed more than the last. Many contained offers to assist with the execution so that she, a Christian mother, would not have to perform it. Others praised her courage and offered her their congratulations for the opportunity to show how a woman was capable of fulfilling the duty of sheriff, no matter what the office entailed. Some were almost too difficult to read, threatening harm to Lillian and her children, telling her she would be committing a grave and unpardonable sin by sending this man to his death, even questioning whether she was fit to care for her children. These were the letters that scared her most of all, the ones she didn't want to read, the ones that made her question what she was doing, despite Father Stuart's comforting words and reassurances.

She grabbed thc top letter from the stack and opened it with the letter opener she had given Everett the first Christmas after he became sheriff. It had been much too extravagant of a gift compared to what they usually exchanged. He had wanted her to return it and get her money back, but she had been so proud of him and had wanted to splurge, to buy him something extra special. Plus, she knew the silver letter opener with its intricately carved handle was something he would use, but would never buy for himself.

She scanned through the letters until she came to one from Arthur Hunt, a former Louisville policeman. Hunt offered to perform the execution, as had many others, but she quickly realized this offer to help was different. He wanted no money in exchange for performing the deed, and he asked her not to tell anyone that he would be involved. Surprised, she realized he seemed to want nothing at all in return for performing the execution - not money, and not fame. He had absolutely nothing to gain by assisting with the execution, and she appreciated his desire for discretion. She moved his letter to the side, planning to write a reply that very afternoon.

The last letter in the stack was from a Judge Wichser in Indianapolis. He recommended she contact a man named Phil Jackson, who had performed an execution he attended several years prior. He emphasized Mr. Jackson's wealth of experience, having performed over fifty executions, and his desire to perform the task in the most humane way possible. Lillian desired the same, and made up her mind to contact this Mr. Jackson, in addition to writing her letter to Mr. Hunt. Perhaps between the two, she could find a way to oversee the execution with a somewhat clear conscience.

CHAPTER THIRTY-TWO - DANIEL

August 1, 1936

Father Wheatley had been visiting Daniel regularly over the past few weeks in his bare cell at the Jefferson County Jail in Louisville. Their first few meetings consisted of Daniel's mumbled, one syllable responses to the priest's questions, but finally, Father Wheatley's persistence paid off. He cracked the hard protective wall that Daniel had built around himself. It was merely a small, hairline fracture in a hard, stone exterior, but Father Wheatley would take what he could get. He prayed without ceasing that Daniel would allow himself to be fully open to the idea of a loving and merciful God who had the power to forgive even the worst of sins.

As the elderly man moved towards the chair across from Daniel, he couldn't help but wonder what would have happened if things had been different, if Daniel had been able to find steady work and resist the temptations that seemed to follow him. What if he had been granted a normal life, with real opportunities and a family to support him?

He settled himself in the creaky wooden chair. "How've you been, my son?"

"I'm good, Father, real good. They've been treatin' me pretty well here, I reckon."

"That's good. I'm glad to hear it," Father Wheatley said with a soft smile.

Daniel swallowed and licked his lips. "It won't be long now, will it?"

Father Wheatley shook his head. "Not much longer, I'm afraid."

Daniel nodded and looked down. He was fidgety, his knee bouncing up and down, his arms crossing and uncrossing. "My lawyer says that we might get a stay from the governor, but if not, I've got about two weeks."

"Yes, that's true." Father Wheatley placed his Bible on the table between them. "Daniel, have you thought any more about what we talked about last week?"

"Yessir. Before we talk about that, though, I was wonderin' if you could tell me somethin.' I been thinkin' long and hard about this, and I don't think the detectives looked hard enough to find Allen McDaniel. I'm thinkin' I might try to get my lawyer to write to some folks and see if they'd be willin' to help search or somethin' to try to find him. Do you think that would work?"

The elderly priest sighed as he stared into Daniel's hopeful eyes, remembering the newspaper articles detailing the lies Daniel told upon his arrest, the wild goose chases he sent the police on, and, of course, the fictional Allen McDaniel, this supposed accomplice he blamed for the attack. Father Wheatley shook his head slowly. "Daniel, I hate to disappoint you, but I think you need to be realistic about your circumstances here."

"Yeah, I know, but if they would just look again, ask some more folks, maybe they could find him. Maybe my lawyers can talk to some folks and get them to start lookin' again."

"What makes you think they would reopen the investigation now?"

"I don't know," Daniel said. "It's hard to explain. I guess when that boy testified at the trial and told them how my foot was hurtin' so bad that day, it got me to thinkin'. I mean, my lawyers didn't seem to pay it no account, but in my mind ... well, I just think they could've asked some more questions, that's all. And if they planted some doubts 'bout me bein' able to climb up on the roof and in and out that window, it ain't too far of a stretch for them jurors to wonder if there musta been someone else there, like I been sayin'."

The priest frowned.

"Look, I know it seems like a waste of time, like I should just give up, but I been fightin' my whole life." Daniel chuckled softly and shook his head. "My sister always used to tell me I don't know when to quit, and I reckon she's tellin' the truth 'bout that. Guess I'll never learn."

Father Wheatley smiled. "I admire your determination, son, really, I do. But I promise you, if there was anything you could say, anything at all, that would change the outcome at this point, I would encourage you to pursue it immediately. But is there? You've already admitted your guilt, both to me and the police. I know it's hard to accept, but sometimes it's okay to quit fighting."

Daniel nodded his head slowly.

"God knows what's in your heart," the priest continued. "It's time to make your peace and ask His forgiveness. That's what matters most. In fact, that's the only thing that matters right now. You have an amazing opportunity here, Daniel. God can use even the worst things in our lives to bring hearts to Him. If you just surrender your life to Him, you can bear witness to the love and mercy of our Lord Jesus Christ."

"You really think so, Father? I mean, you really think He'd forgive me after everything?" His voice was barely a whisper.

"I know it, as surely as I know the sun will come up each day. It's time to stop fighting, Daniel. It's time to accept responsibility for what happened and make your peace with God."

And suddenly, just like that, he knew.

Like a lightbulb coming on and illuminating a darkened room, Daniel felt a sense of calm and peace flooding through his body. The old priest was right. He couldn't explain how, but he knew. It didn't matter at this point if he told the police or his lawyers anything else. It didn't matter if they knew the details, the how and why it happened. His fate had been sealed when he signed the confession, and even more so when the jury handed over his sentence. Why would the governor change his mind now? Anything he said at this point would just be viewed as a desperate attempt by a desperate man to avoid a punishment he deserved. And honestly, he knew he did deserve it. No matter what had happened in Suzanne

Bower's bedroom or who else was involved that night, one fact remained. He may not have killed her, but if it were not for him, she would still be alive. Nothing he said now could change that.

But if what the elderly priest told him was true, God would forgive all his sins - even the ones that had blackened his heart to the point he wasn't sure it would ever be clean again. He could be washed clean.

No more running.

No more hiding.

Only peace.

A small flicker of hope sparked within him. Not hope that his sentence would be changed and his life would be spared, but hope that there was something more, something bigger, something beyond the burdens of this life.

"Maybe you're right, Father," Daniel said, "as long as you're sure it's not too late for me."

Father Wheatley smiled and felt his heart fill with compassion for this young man and love for a God whose mercy was never-ending, never failing. He smiled as he reached out to put a hand on Daniel's shoulder. "Son, it's never too late."

CHAPTER THIRTY-THREE - LILLIAN

August 2, 1936

"Mother, what's this all about?" Mary asked.

The supper dishes had been cleared away, but she had asked the children to remain at the table a few minutes longer. She looked around at them, and at the empty chair across from her that they had not been able to bring themselves to remove. It stood like a silent sentinel at each and every meal, a reminder that this family was no longer whole.

She took a breath and prayed silently for the Lord to help her keep her voice steady. As hard as this conversation was going to be, it would be that much harder if she lost control of her emotions.

"I need to talk to you all about something important, and it may be difficult to hear."

The children glanced at one another and then back at her, wide-eyed. She hated what she was about to say, hated that they had to have this difficult conversation.

"As you know, Daniel Porter's sentence is due to be carried out in less than two weeks," she began. "The hanging will take place downtown, and as sheriff, it is my duty to oversee things and ensure that everything goes according to plan."

"Will we be able to go? Tommy said his father is taking him and they may even camp out the night before so they can get a good view," Patrick said eagerly.

"Absolutely not!" Lillian replied, perhaps a little too forcefully. She softened her tone and tried again. "No, Patrick, you children will not be attending the execution. It is no place for women and children to be."

"But you'll be there, mother. If it's no place for women and children, why do you have to go?" Even at eight years old, James was often the most logical thinker of the bunch.

"Because of a statute, James."

"A statue?"

She smiled. "No, son, a statute. S-T-A-T-U-T-E. That's a special state law. This particular law says that the acting sheriff must oversee the execution in the county in which the crime occurred. I'm the acting sheriff, so that means it's my responsibility."

"But do you have to?" Worry was etched on Jack's face. As the man of the house now, she knew he felt an innate need to protect them all, to protect even his mother whenever he could. "Can't they make an exception in this case? I mean, it's not like you asked for any of this."

"Believe me, if there was any way for me to be relieved of this duty, I would seek it out in a heartbeat. I've turned it over and over in my mind, but there's no other option. I must fulfill my duty. It's what's expected." She paused and released a long sigh. "It's what your father would have done."

"Yes, but that's different. What will people say if our mother hangs a man in front of the whole town?" Mary said in a quiet voice, and Lillian looked at her, realizing it was a question she had probably been wanting to ask for weeks. It was most assuredly a question Lillian had been asking herself since the moment she sat in that crowded courtroom and heard the jury foreman read Daniel Porter's sentence.

"I don't know," Lillian answered honestly. Her eyes filled, and she took several deep breaths before forcing the words out. "I can't tell you what people will say about me, or about you, or our friends and family, for that matter. But I do feel that it's best if you all leave Waverly for awhile, just until things calm down."

They sat in stunned silence until James, wide-eyed, said, "Leave Waverly? But where will we go?"

"Well, I've spoken with Father Stuart, and he wrote a letter on our behalf to the boys' school in Bardstown. There's no way I could afford tuition for all three of you to attend, but Father Stuart explained our unusual situation, and the dean of students at the school agreed to waive the fees so that you can enroll there." She looked at them each in turn, but they seemed too stunned to speak. "You'll be well taken care of, I promise. This is a very well-respected school. This could be a great opportunity for you boys," she added hopefully, even though she felt as if her heart was being ripped out of her chest. How could she possibly send them away? Was this really the best solution? Was she protecting them, or only causing more pain to these children who had already lost so much?

"But Mother, I don't want to leave. I don't want to leave my friends or my school or our house," James said, tears spilling down his cheeks. Jack stood and walked to him, putting his arm around his little brother's shoulders. Lillian took deep breaths and swallowed, afraid if she opened her mouth, the sob she was holding back would come raging out. She longed to gather little James in her arms, to smooth his hair down and squeeze him tight, to protect him, to protect all of them, from what may lie ahead.

"It's okay, little man." Jack squeezed his little brother's shoulders. "Think of it as a grand adventure."

His words hung in the silent air until Mary whispered, "What about me, Mother?"

Lillian looked down at the floral tablecloth before answering, desperately trying to block out James's sniffling and the look of betrayal in Patrick's brown eyes. "I've spoken to your great aunt, Martha, in Johnsville. She's agreed to take you in, Mary. She has plenty of space now that it's just her in that house, and she'd love the company."

"I see."

Lillian slowly looked up, and the pain reflected on her beautiful daughter's face nearly broke her resolve.

"It's for the best," she said, hoping to make them see, to make them understand that the last thing she wanted to do was to rip her fragile family apart even more. That everything she had done and would do in the future was done only out of love and a desire to protect them. That they were her entire world now, and she wasn't sure she would survive being apart from them. Sending them away, even if it killed her, was the only way to protect them from the gossip, the threats, the danger seeping through Waverly like a poison.

"When do we leave?" Patrick sounded so much like Everett that Lillian's heart seemed to stop for a moment.

"Tuesday morning."

"So soon?" Mary asked.

"Yes, I think the sooner the better. Father Stuart will drive the boys to Bardstown that morning, and Deputy Mitchell has agreed to take you to Johnsville that afternoon once his shift is over."

She looked at each of them in turn. She hoped she was doing the right thing. She hoped they would be strong. She hoped she could survive being apart from them. Most of all, she fervently hoped they would be sheltered from the madness that was soon to descend on Waverly.

CHAPTER THIRTY-FOUR - SARAH

July 7, 2006

Steve twirled another forkful of pasta, chewed thoughtfully, and reached for the last piece of buttery garlic bread in the basket between us. "So, you still haven't figured anything out, huh?"

"Nope. I tried calling him yesterday, but he wasn't feeling very well. He sounded tired, so I didn't even bring it up. I feel like I don't talk to him often enough, and then when I do, I don't want to talk about this case the whole time. I keep having to remind myself that he's ninety years old, for God's sake." I delicately tore off a piece of garlic bread and dabbed it in the alfredo sauce pooled at the edge of my plate.

Steve signaled our server for a refill on the garlic bread before answering, "Well, I'm sure he finds the whole thing unpleasant to remember. It's crazy, the idea of going to watch an execution like it's some kind of show or circus event. It seems so ... I don't know, inhumane or something. I mean, who really wants to watch something like that?"

"I know. But it was a different time, I guess. I mean, obviously a lot of people wanted to see it because there were thousands that showed up for it. I read in one of the articles that the execution was originally going to be on the courthouse lawn, but they had just planted some shrubs and flowers all around there. I guess someone at the sheriff's department didn't want the crowds messing up the new landscaping. They built the scaffold in an empty lot by the county garage so there'd be more room for people who were coming to watch."

Steve shook his head and chewed a mouth full of pasta before continuing. "I wonder if your grandfather had a good view. I mean, I know that sounds weird, but I wonder if he was, like, really close to the gallows or something, and that's why it's so hard for him to talk about."

"You know, you could be right. I would think seeing something like that up close would definitely have an impact on you."

"Yeah who knows? He may have been traumatized by it or had some kind of PTSD from it."

"Could be," I shrugged. "Oh, there is this one weird thing I found when I was reading the other day that I forgot to tell you about. It seems Daniel Porter injured his foot right before the murder happened. I'm not sure how bad it was, and it may not even matter, but I thought it was interesting. Mark thought it was strange, too. This twelve year old boy testified that he clearly saw him limping that afternoon, and Porter told him he had dropped an iron on his foot earlier that day."

"Really? That's weird. Didn't you tell me he climbed up on a roof or did some kind of crazy acrobatics to get to the old lady's window?"

"Exactly! I don't know how he could've gotten up there if his foot was hurt that badly. It's so strange that his attorneys didn't even follow up or pursue it. The kid mentioned it in his testimony, and then nothing else was said about it. It seems like his defense could have at least tried to use it to mount a plausible defense."

He nodded as the server placed another basket of garlic bread on the table.

"Can I get you anything else?"

Steve glanced at my empty glass. "I think the lady would like some more wine, please."

"Certainly, sir." The waiter nodded as he scurried off.

"More wine?" I grinned. "Are you trying to get me drunk, Mr. Harper?"

"Absolutely," he answered with a wink. "So what else? Did you find any other interesting clues?"

"Well, I did find out how they first learned Daniel Porter was a suspect. According to this one newspaper article, some girl turned him in."

"Oh, really? Who was she?"

"I have no idea." I waited while the server refilled my wine glass. "Her name wasn't listed in the article. It said that a young girl who worked at a tavern spoke to the police and gave them a tip that Daniel might be involved. I think she also helped them find him because it said the deputies arrested him outside the same tavern where this girl worked - Tugg's, or Tieg's, or something like that. The girl never testified at the trial, though, and I can't find out anything else about her. I don't even know her name. It's like she just disappeared."

"Sounds like another mystery for Detective Sarah Harper to solve." He smiled and raised his wineglass in a little toast. "Well, I, for one, am proud of you for sticking with this."

I smiled, lifting my own glass and gently clinking it against his. "Thanks, honey. I have to say, I'm pretty proud of myself for sticking with it, too. Besides, it's been fun to have something like this to occupy my time while you've been gone."

Steve put his wineglass down, suddenly serious. He carefully wiped his mouth on his linen napkin, then reached across the table to take my hand.

"I know things haven't been easy for you, Sarah," he said quietly. "I know it's probably been even harder to deal with everything with me being gone so much. I want you to know I'm sorry I haven't been there for you."

His eyes searched mine, and I could feel my cheeks flushing, my heart beating faster.

"I know you said you're not ready, that you need more time, but I feel like you're not even willing to talk to me about it," he said, frowning. "When you shut down instead of dealing with it, that makes it worse. It makes it harder on both of us. I can't just pretend nothing happened and hope it'll go away. You have to talk to me."

I looked down at our hands still joined together, laying on the white tablecloth. I felt my head shaking slowly, my eyes filling with tears.

I had failed him in so many ways, failed us both, and here I was, failing again. Failing to find the words to explain, failing to tell him how I wanted nothing more than to give him what he wanted, how he deserved so much more than I could give him. And yet, the fear gripped me like a vise. I couldn't go through it again, at least not yet. The joy, the excitement and anticipation, and then the pain and fear, the loss so tangible, I felt as if the doctor had literally taken away a part of me, had scraped out my identity, my hope, along with everything else. I couldn't go back there. I couldn't take that chance again. Not to mention the sympathetic looks from family, a steady stream of awkward conversations with those who hadn't heard, the apologies, the empty offers to help out. "If there's anything you need, just let us know."

Anything we need?

What we need is our baby.

What we need is for my body not to betray me.

My fragile heart had been shattered in that sterile hospital room. It had not yet been pieced back together, and I wondered if it ever would.

All these thoughts raced through my brain, and yet when I looked into my husband's worried eyes, I could only manage five little words.

"I'm sorry," I whispered, shaking my head. "I just can't."

CHAPTER THIRTY-FIVE - DANIEL

August 13, 1936

Daniel watched the trees flying by the window in a blur as the black Ford flew down the highway. A hot wind blew through the car, and he was thankful for the fresh air, hot as it was. The deputies in the front seat carried on an easy conversation about the ongoing heat wave and the Yankees' chances in the World Series. The noise of the wind whipping through the vehicle meant Daniel could only catch about every fifth word, so he had given up on trying to follow their conversation miles ago.

He suddenly realized the young officer in the front passenger seat must have spoken to him. He had turned sideways and was looking expectantly back at Daniel over the seat. Daniel noticed a small nick on his chin, the blood now scabbed over, and wondered if he had cut himself shaving that morning.

"I'm sorry, sir. I didn't hear you," Daniel nearly shouted to be heard over the wind roaring through the car's windows.

"I said, boy, you're creating quite a commotion down in Waverly. I ain't never seen nothin' like it."

"How so, sir?" Daniel asked, confused.

"Well, I reckon people all over have been followin' your case. There are reporters in town from Louisville, Frankfort, heck, from all over the state. The hotels are all full. I heard tell that some of them out of town folks are sleepin' in their cars, and a lot of folks in Waverly are offerin' beds and even floor space up for rent at their houses for those that couldn't get in one of the hotels," he said.

"Rentin' out floor space, you say? I swan," the other officer said, shaking his head in disbelief.

"Why would folks do all that?" Daniel asked, confused.

The young officer looked uncomfortable, no doubt wishing he had not spoken to Daniel at all. "Well, you know, I guess folks have been followin' things with your case in the papers for so long... and, of course, pretty much everybody in Waverly knew Mrs. Suzanne Bower. I gather she was well respected." He shrugged. "So, anyway, people have been following the stories about the trial and all, and now they plan to come watch ..." the deputy trailed off. He looked at the officer next to him as if hoping to be rescued from the awkward turn this conversation had taken, but the driver merely stared at the road ahead. "Well, you know ..." the deputy continued carefully, "to see things through to the end, so to speak."

"Oh," Daniel said. "I see."

The officers sat in silence for a moment until the driver asked if the deputy had seen the latest Spencer Tracy picture.

Daniel blocked out their chatter and focused on watching the trees and the occasional farm as they passed by, trying to remember every detail and commit them to his memory. Was that the last farmhouse he would ever see? Were those the last cows he would ever see gathered around a pond? His eyes felt dry from the hot wind and his reluctance to blink, afraid he would miss something. He had taken many things for granted. Fresh air. Trees.

And Sally. Oh, he had taken her for granted for so long. He wondered where she was and what she was doing at that exact moment. Hurting Sally - that was something he never wanted or intended to do. She certainly never deserved it. She did nothing but love him when he was at his worst, and how did he pay her back? With bruises and shouting and getting her all tangled up in a murder investigation, that's how. He shook his head in disgust.

They passed an old country church sitting on a hill. Daniel looked at the cross perched high atop the steeple, then reached up to grasp the small gold cross hanging delicately from the chain around his neck. He absently rubbed the pendant between his thumb and index finger. When Father Wheatley fastened the cross around Daniel's neck on the day of his baptism just days earlier, a calmness flooded through him. Daniel had not taken it off since, even when he laid down on his cot to sleep.

Father Wheatley promised him during one of their meetings there was no sin too great for God to forgive, no matter how terrible or unforgivable it seemed. He knew he had a whole stack of sins, some far worse than others, and he was sure glad to hear God could forgive him of all of them.

He hoped that one day, maybe a long time from now, Sally could forgive him, too.

PART 4

THE PUNISHMENT

CHAPTER THIRTY-SIX - LILLIAN

August 13, 1936

The sheriff stood behind her desk and looked at the grim faces surrounding her. In addition to her deputies and other officers lining the walls, two FBI agents stood just inside the doorway.

No one spoke.

The two chairs across from her desk were occupied by Phil Jackson, the official hangman who would oversee the proceedings, and Arthur Hunt, who had arrived from Louisville that morning.

Mr. Hunt, a small, pale man whose suit looked much too large for his frame, was twirling his hat around and around in his fingers, his wide eyes darting from side to side. Lillian had spoken with Mitchell the night before, expressing her concerns about Hunt's ability to follow through and pull the lever on the gallows when the time came, but Mitchell assured her things would go well, that Hunt was a former police officer, after all. Lillian could only hope he was right. If Hunt failed, it would be up to her, as acting sheriff, to pull the lever. She shuddered at the thought.

Mitchell stepped forward. "Ma'am, I think everyone is here."

She nodded and took a deep breath. "Right. Okay, let's get started, gentlemen. We have a lot to go over, as I'm sure you know. First of all, I must ask you for your discretion. Mr. Hunt has understandably asked that his identity remain a secret. These reporters are ruthless and have been hounding us for weeks, but please respect his wishes to keep quiet about his involvement. I have not indicated to anyone who will pull the lever when the time comes, and I expect you to do the same up until the moment of execution."

"Thank you kindly, ma'am," Hunt said, nodding to her. He turned in his chair to look at the men standing behind him. "I hope ya'll can understand why I'd want it kept out of the papers. I'm surely glad to be of service, but that don't mean I want my family name tarnished 'cause of it."

Lillian thought of the death threats and letters full of personal attacks she had received. She certainly couldn't blame the man.

"Now, Mr. Jackson," she continued, "we will begin with you. Please walk us through step by step, as you are far more experienced than the rest of us in matters such as this. Gentlemen, give Mr. Jackson your undivided attention. I cannot begin to express to you the importance that everything go according to plan. We can't afford to make any mistakes."

"Certainly, Sheriff," Phil Jackson replied as he stood to speak. His tone was serious, yet confident. Sheriff Conner felt certain she could trust him to orchestrate things, even if Hunt had her worried.

"The most important thing is for death to occur quickly and humanely," he said. "There will be a very large crowd, perhaps the largest you've ever seen, surrounding the gallows. It is possible, from what I've gathered, that the crowd may even spill into the side streets surrounding the fence around the lot. In order for things to go smoothly, we must perform our duties like a well-oiled machine, gentlemen. There is absolutely no room for error." He looked at each of them in turn, ensuring they understood the gravity of the task at hand. Lillian thought she noticed his gaze lingering on Hunt a moment longer than the rest.

"You will signal to me when it's time, won't you, Mr. Jackson?" Hunt suddenly asked, and Lillian noted the slight tremor in his voice. She had also noted the small flask he had been sipping from discreetly just before the meeting began.

"Yes, Mr. Hunt. I will fit the rope around the criminal's neck, ensuring the knot is behind his left ear. This will allow his neck to break quickly when the trap is sprung." He gestured behind his ear and then made a swift breaking motion with his hands. Deputy Mitchell flinched, and Lillian gasped and covered her mouth with her hand involuntarily. She quickly dropped it back down to her side, hoping no one had noticed.

"Once the rope is secure and in place around Porter's neck," Jackson continued, "I will turn to you, Mr. Hunt, and then I will nod. That will be your signal. I don't find that giving a verbal command everyone can hear is necessary. I think it's more humane if the condemned man doesn't realize when the exact moment of death will occur, you see."

"I reckon that makes sense," Hunt said, nodding. "So, I just pull the lever when you have the rope secure, is that right?"

Mr. Jackson eyed Hunt wearily and said, "Mr. Hunt, again, I must implore you to fulfill your duty as charged. You will wait for my nod, and then, and only then, will you pull the lever. Not a moment before."

"Yes, sir," Hunt said, his eyes darting around the room at the other officers.

"Once the trap opens and he falls, we will wait for the doctor to pronounce the time of death. I can tell you from my experience that it will seem like an excruciatingly long time, gentlemen, but it's important that you all remain at your assigned posts until the doctor has pronounced him gone, no matter what happens."

Lillian noticed the officers nodding solemnly. "We can't have the crowd rushing the gallows or otherwise engaging in mob behavior," she said, feeling the need to emphasize Jackson's point. "Everyone must be on their guard at all times. We don't know how the crowd will react. We have been granted assistance from our fellow officers in Jefferson County, Rogersville, and the FBI regional field office, but as Mr. Jackson has indicated, the crowd will be substantial. We'll need all hands on deck until it's finished and the body has been removed."

Hunt looked around the room, then cleared his throat and asked, "Where will they take him? After, I mean."

There was an uncomfortable silence, and then Deputy Mitchell spoke softly. "The funeral home for coloreds on Fourth Street will take care of removing the body. I've told them to be sure and leave the hood on until they take him away. We don't want the crowd to see the face of death." His words seemed to hang in the air a moment before fading away.

"Well, I guess that's it, then," Lillian said with a sigh, hoping she wasn't forgetting anything. "I will be present during the execution in order to fulfill my duty as Sheriff of Clay County, but I plan to wait in a car near the gallows in order to avoid the reporters." She turned and looked at each officer as she spoke. "I am putting my faith in you all, gentlemen, to see this through to the end. Our duty is to ensure it will be done swiftly, humanely, and that the good people of this county know that justice has been served."

They thanked her and quietly filed out, each man lost in his own anxious thoughts, until Lillian found herself standing alone in the empty office. She sat in the old wooden chair behind the desk and put her head in her hands. She wondered how many times her husband, bearing the burden of this office, had sat in this very chair and strained under the weight of his role as sheriff. She glanced down at the desk. Had he placed his elbows in these very spots? Or on the arms of this chair? She looked at the swirls in the wood on the desk in front of her and slowly traced the patterns with her fingers, imagining his calloused fingers doing the same, until the tears threatened to spill over.

She got to her feet, took a deep breath, and wiped her eyes. With shaking fingers, she smoothed back her hair and straightened the badge pinned to her dress. Then, she walked to the hallway and down the stairs, making her way to Daniel Porter's cell.

CHAPTER THIRTY-SEVEN - DANIEL

August 13, 1936

Daniel immediately knew who she was, of course. Waverly was not that big of a town.

The young deputy with her pulled the key ring from his belt loop and unlocked Daniel's cell without speaking. He pulled the heavy door to the side as she approached. Daniel stood up from his cot, not sure what he was supposed to do. They had told him to finish his dinner and that they would come for him early in the morning. Why was she here? And why now? Was he going somewhere? Was he being moved to another cell? A sudden glimmer of hope flashed through him. Had there been a call from the governor? Father Wheatley had told him the governor was the only one with the authority to delay his execution.

"Hello, Daniel." Her soft voice echoed and seemed out of place in the dimly lit cell. Her eyes roamed the small cell, taking in the cot, the sink and toilet in the corner, the low ceiling.

“Ma'am." He nodded a greeting at her, surprised that she had called him by his first name as if they were old friends and she had stopped by for a chat. He glanced around his cell at the meager furnishings, trying to see them as she was seeing them. What thoughts must be running through her mind? He wasn't sure whether he should invite her to sit down, or stand and wait. He felt awkward and stiff, his heart hammering in his chest. He was surprised she couldn't hear it in the silence that hung between them.

"I just ... " she hesitated before continuing, "well, I just wanted to see if there's anything you need. Before tomorrow, I mean."

When he didn't answer, she turned and placed her hands around the bars of his cell, squeezing tightly, her knuckles turning white. He imagined those delicate white hands slipping a noose over his neck.

"I can't imagine what you're thinking right now," she continued. "Do you need something else to eat, or some more paper? Deputy Mitchell said you wanted to write a letter to your sister. I can bring you more paper."

He stood in shocked silence, unsure of how to respond. Finally, he cleared his throat and picked up a folded sheet of paper from his cot. "No, ma'am, thank you kindly. I finished writin' this here letter to my sister, and I ain't got no one else to write to. I'd be much obliged if you could see it gets mailed to her, though." He noticed her hand shaking slightly as she took the folded sheet of paper from him.

When she looked at him, the intensity of her gaze made his breath catch. Her quiet words came out in a rushed whisper and filled the space between them. "Daniel, I want you to know that I'll do what I can to make this as easy on you as possible."

He nodded his head, marveling at the wonder of it all. In less than 12 hours, this woman would be the one to end his life, and yet here she stood in his cell, sounding for all the world like she was trying to comfort him. He looked at her mouth and imagined those lips asking him if he had any last words. He looked into her blue eyes, wondering if hers would be the last he would look into tomorrow before meeting his Maker. This woman, who was now offering to bring him some extra food or provide whatever she could to ease his fear, would tomorrow decide the moment, the exact second, his life ended. She would decide which breath would be his last on this earth. His life, his very soul, was in her small, delicate hands.

"I also wanted you to know that we have a man who is very experienced in these kind of things," she said. "He's promised it'll be over quick. I haven't told anyone besides my officers, but I want you to know. I won't be the one to..." she stopped, swallowed, and then continued. "I won't be the one to do it. It won't be me."

He nodded, unsure of how to respond.

"Do you need some different clothes?"

He blinked. "Ma'am?"

"Do you need some clothes or anything?" she asked again.

He stared at her. He couldn't think of a thing she could do for him, but maybe it would make things easier on them both if she brought him something, just some small thing. He thought quickly and glanced around his empty cell, racking his brain. He looked down at his feet.

"Well, ma'am, do you think I could get some clean socks? These are mighty dirty," he said softly as he lifted his trouser leg and indicated his once white cotton socks, now tinged a light gray. It seemed a strange request, even to his own ears, but he couldn't think of anything else to say.

He waited quietly, and yet to his surprise, she didn't laugh, didn't mock him in the slightest.

"Clean socks? Well, of course. Of course we can do that. I'll see to it that they're brought to you right away," she replied, nodding.

"Thank you, ma'am," he said.

"You're welcome, Daniel." She looked at him a moment longer and then turned to go.

The deputy locked the door behind her, and Daniel lay on the cot listening to her footsteps down the hall, which seemed to echo long after she was gone.

CHAPTER THIRTY-EIGHT - LILLIAN

August 14, 1936

It was larger than she had imagined. The platform itself towered nearly twenty feet above the heads of the massive crowd of onlookers, the crossbeam stretching across the dark sky above it.

She had walked across that wooden platform the evening before, after her conversation with Daniel Porter in his cell. She had stood very still and looked out at the spectators who were already arriving, all hoping to get a good spot for the event.

"What time is it, ma'am?" Officer Tompkins interrupted her thoughts as he maneuvered between the people crowding the streets in order to park the car on the side street by the county garage.

She glanced at the watch pin on her dress, her last Christmas gift from Everett. "Half past four," she replied in a quiet voice.

She looked down at the small notecard in her hand filled Jackson's instructions. Her hand trembled so much that her neat, looping handwriting was a blur of tangled letters. It was no matter. She had read the step by step instructions so many times, the words seemed permanently tattooed on her brain.

Step 1: Arrive at 4:30 and wait in car on Locust Street

She had wanted Deputy Mitchell to be the one to drive her, but decided at the last minute he needed to be on the platform instead. She trusted him more than any of her other men, and it helped slightly calm her frayed nerves to know he would be there at the center of the action in case something went wrong.

Step 2: Jackson arrives with ladder to prepare rope and test trap

Jackson had assured her again that morning that things would go smoothly, the rope would be properly prepared, and the trap tested again before time to begin. She appreciated his confidence, but she also knew her insides would not stop quaking until it was all over.

Step 3: Officers escort criminal to gallows

She had planned to go see Daniel again this morning, had even found herself standing at the top of the stairs, but her feet had suddenly felt glued to the floor. She had stood there, swallowing her fear, her uncertainties. What could she say to him at this point?

Deputy Mitchell had stood behind her, patiently waiting, before whispering, "Ma'am, it's okay if you don't want to see him. He's made his peace. We're all ready. Things will be fine."

She looked at Mitchell and nodded, unable to hide the relief in her face. "Yes, I suppose you're right. We had best get to it."

She had walked away from the stairs leading to Daniel Porter, who at that very moment was sitting silent and still on his cot, waiting for what was to come.

Step 4: At Jackson's signal, Hunt will pull the lever to spring the trap.

This was the part she had worried about, the part that had kept her from getting any sleep the restless night before. What if Hunt couldn't do it? What if he was as unreliable as she feared? She briefly contemplated asking another officer to step in and take his place, but she hated the thought of burdening another man with such a terrible duty. No, it was her responsibility. As much as the thought tore her apart, she knew deep down that if Hunt failed, it would be up to her as acting sheriff to take over and see things through to the end.

She stared down at the instructions, everything clearly spelled out like her recipe for Everett's favorite peach cobbler. All they had to do was follow four simple steps, and things would turn out fine.

She marveled at the throngs surrounding the wooden framework of the gallows. The lot was already full, and spectators spilled out into the streets. The fence gate on Locust had been opened to allow more viewers to squeeze into the lot, and she was startled to see silhouettes of men, their outlines highlighted by the moon, watching the proceedings from the rooftops of the county garage and Koll's Grocery. She knew without a doubt she had never seen so many people in her life. The darkness prevented her from seeing the full extent of the crowds, and yet the low rumble of voices seemed to stretch for several blocks.

She looked back at the gallows and remembered standing on the platform the day before, glancing down at the small white letter X marking the spot on the trap door. A mark to let Daniel know where to stand, much like a small mark placed on stage during a performance to let the actors know their marks.

Is that what this is to them? she wondered, looking out over the crowd. A performance? A show? A drama to be played out in front of a crowd of spectators? This audience of men who came to see the climactic end to this tragedy would go home to their wives and families and jobs and farms, with a story to tell and a memory that would fade with time. But not her. She knew that she would never forget a moment of this day.

Several reporters noticed her sitting in the darkened car and hurried over, notepads in hand and pencils at the ready. They crowded around the window like dogs begging for scraps from the table.

"Madam Sheriff, is it true you're going to pull the lever on the gallows?"

She took a breath, smoothed the skirt of her navy blue dress, turned slowly, and forced her voice to remain clear and calm. "I shall not reveal anything until the time comes, gentlemen."

Disappointed, they stood looking at one another, as if trying to decide what question to ask next. Officer Tompkins made the decision for them when he turned, leaned back over the seat, and called to them out the rear window, "How about you fellers move along now and give Sheriff Conner some space?"

Reluctantly, the reporters turned and headed back towards the crowd. As they retreated, she heard them begin arguing about which vantage point would give them an unobstructed view, but also a quick getaway so they could file their stories.

"Ma'am, is this okay?" Tompkins asked, and at first she wasn't sure what he was referring to.

"I think we're close enough you can oversee things, but I can also cut down Locust if we need to leave in a hurry," he continued, waving his hand to indicate which direction they could make their escape.

Oh, if only she could really escape this nightmare.

"Yes, Tompkins," she answered, her voice barely a whisper. She cleared her throat and tried again, louder this time. "Yes, Tompkins, this is fine. Thank you." She looked down at her lap and saw that, in her nervousness, she had shredded Jackson's notecard of instructions into dozens of tiny scraps of paper.

CHAPTER THIRTY-NINE - SALLY

August 14, 1936

Sally pressed her forehead to the window of her small, second-floor bedroom above the tavern. She felt like the room, and indeed her whole world, was spinning out of control.

She could see the focal point clearly across the street, along with the throngs of noisy onlookers jostling for a better view. The structure rose high into the air, a huge contraption composed of smooth, sharp lines and angles towering over the crowd. The platform itself was smaller than she had imagined, and it seemed a novelty to her that the entire thing didn't collapse under the weight of the sturdy frame and giant crossbeam above.

She was eternally grateful to Hershel for allowing her to hide out here during the trial. The one time he caught Daniel sneaking out of her room in the early morning hours, he had made his disapproval known. But she told him days later she had broken things off with Daniel, and he believed her. Once the trial ended, she found herself hanging on to her sanity with tenuous threads and feared she would collapse from the pressing weight of guilt that haunted her day and night.

Hershel's growing concern had been well-founded, and when he demanded an explanation as to why she was moping around the tavern and neglecting her duties, she had collapsed and sobbed in his arms. She told him about her overwhelming guilt, about how she felt the eyes of every customer boring into her as she wiped the counters at the Tavern, the whispers exchanged over beer mugs, the nods in her direction from the regulars, as if they could see disloyalty and untrustworthiness painted right across her face.

Hershel had been sympathetic from the start. He had always viewed Sally like the daughter he never had, and though he was disappointed that she had ever gotten involved with a no good criminal like Daniel Porter, he also knew it was not her fault. Daniel had taken advantage of her innocence and tricked her into believing his lies. Hershel did not judge her in the least. Instead, he agreed to handle the lunch and dinner crowds on his own with the new girl, Della, so that Sally could stay out of sight. If any of the regulars asked, he would tell them Sally had not been feeling well and was resting. In the meantime, she could rest in her room during the day and help him with cleaning, washing dishes, and food prep in the evenings, once the tavern closed and the questioning glances and whispers were long gone. It was hard on him to handle things on his own with just Della, who was inexperienced and slow, but he managed. Sally knew she could never repay him for his kindness.

The sun was starting to rise, and the sky was a beautiful yellow gold, with a few wispy clouds. She knew the heat would be stifling by that afternoon, but for the moment, the glass of the window felt smooth and cool against her skin.

Suddenly, the steady, low buzzing of the crowd became silent as a tomb, and she watched in awe as a path formed in the middle of the throngs of people. There were no officers telling the bystanders to step aside; there was no jostling of the crowd. It was as if they had rehearsed their parts and knew instinctively where and how and when to move.

Once the path was clear, there was hardly any movement among the crowd, as if they were holding their breath. All eyes turned in one silent, fluid motion toward the south side of the lot.

She saw the bobbing heads of some police officers in their dark uniforms walking up the path through the crowd. And then she saw him.

Her breath caught in her throat as she pressed her face closer to the glass and took in his bright white shirt, freshly pressed and carefully buttoned to the top. A small, sad smile played at her lips as she wondered who had ironed his shirt for him, or if they allowed him to iron his own clothes one last time.

She marveled at how small he looked standing between the two taller officers, almost like a child.

He shuffled slightly as he walked, his normal gliding way of moving now gone. She wondered briefly if his injured foot was still bothering him that much. She wondered if she should have written to him. She wondered what he would have said to her. She put a hand on her swollen stomach. She wondered if she should have told him everything.

But what good would it have done? There was no future for him, and certainly no future for her if she stayed here in Waverly, a young, single black woman with a child on the way, a child whose father was a convicted murderer.

Still, she wondered if he could have at least forgiven her. A wave of nausea came over her as she imagined for the thousandth time the betrayal he must have felt. She clung desperately, fervently to the hope that Daniel had not known it was her, that he had not realized she told the police they would find him in the alley that day, that instead he thought it was just a coincidence that they stumbled upon him there.

She reached into her apron pocket, took out a piece of peppermint hard candy, and popped it into her mouth, hoping it would calm her roiling stomach.

"Oh, Daniel, how did we come to this?" she whispered, closing her eyes for a brief moment.

When the officers and Daniel reached the base of the gallows, she saw them pause. Daniel said something to the officer on his left, who nodded his head. The officers stepped aside, and Daniel turned around facing the onlookers. At first, Sally thought maybe he was going to make a speech, to admit his sins or perhaps try to proclaim his innocence. Maybe he would speak harsh words to the crowd, shaming them for their desire to gather here and watch a man die on stage like it was some kind of tragic play. But as the stunned crowd watched in silence, Daniel Porter surprised them all. He sat on the wooden steps, the gallows looming behind him, and carefully removed his shoes and dirty socks. While thousands of confused onlookers watched in silence, he pulled out a fresh, clean pair of white socks from a side pocket.

Tears now spilled freely down Sally's cheeks, even as she smiled. She saw the stares of the crowd and imagined what the reporters would say about Daniel's actions. And yet, she knew it fit him perfectly. Of course he would want clean socks.

Once he finished changing his socks, he stood slowly, his head down. He looked up at the crowd for a moment and then turned his gaze toward the tavern. Sally took a step back, her hand to her mouth. She could have sworn he was looking right at her. She had to hold on to the edge of the table beside her with both hands to keep from collapsing to the floor.

In that moment, that one breath, she imagined what their life could have been. A life away from this place, away from Waverly, away from the judgment of others who misunderstood him, away from the accusations and the lies that made him angry, the struggles that caused his temper to explode. Just she and Daniel and their child. She felt sure the baby was a boy. And now he would be a boy who would never know his daddy, never have a father there to teach him to fish and hunt and how to be a man.

A choked sob escaped her as she thought of the absolute unfairness of it all.

She looked back as Daniel turned and said something to the officers standing beside him at the bottom of the steps. The officers nodded and stepped forward, one on each side, grasped his elbows, and helped him mount the steps. Sally counted each step as he marched up. One, two, three...

She glanced at the clock on the wall. 5:25. It was almost time. Another wave of nausea hit her and she struggled to keep herself together, closing her eyes and breathing deeply until it passed. She wasn't sure she could watch, and yet she could not look away, could not close her eyes. She would see this through to the end.

CHAPTER FORTY- DANIEL

August 14, 1936

He stood at the top of the steps for a moment, officers on either side of him firmly clutching his elbows. He wasn't sure if they were there to help him keep his balance as he came up the steps in shackles, or to keep him from collapsing at the top if he lost his nerve.

The small platform was crowded, mostly with people that he didn't recognize. He was glad to see Father Wheatley there. The elderly priest's eyes were sad, but he managed a heartfelt smile and nod at Daniel. A tall man in a dark jacket nodded at him, too, and then Daniel's breath caught in his throat when he glanced down at the man's hands and saw the black hood clutched there.

Daniel looked out over the huge crowd. He felt as if he were standing on a raft floating in a sea of white faces, all peering up at him. Some of the faces were familiar to him, but many more were not. He recognized Mr. Koll from the grocery near the front, and Hershel Tiegg from the tavern where Sally worked standing next to him. Mr. Anderson was not far behind them, his expression blank.

Despite its large size, the crowd was absolutely silent.

He looked in the direction of Tieggs' Tavern. He had not heard from Sally, and though it broke his heart, he knew it was for the best. Still, he couldn't help wondering if she was watching somewhere, if maybe she was standing at that bedroom window right now, peering out at him. The sun glaring off the glass of the building's windows made it impossible for him to tell.

The tall man stepped a little closer to him. "Do you have any last words?"

He thought for a moment. He had not prepared a statement. In fact, until that moment, he had not even thought of what his last words should be. What do you say when you know you will never speak again, when it's the last time your voice will ever be heard by another human being this side of eternity?

He thought frantically, but could think of no great words of wisdom, no phrase for the reporters to put in their stories, no message for the masses gathered in front of him. What more was there to say now, anyway?

"No, sir. I've made my peace with God. I just want to say I'm sorry for everything, and I guess I don't have nothin' else to say 'sides that."

"Well, all right then. It's time," the man said with a nod.

Daniel took a deep breath. He hoped he would be able to remain standing on his own. He did not want to collapse while all these white people stared up at him, but his knees were shaking so much that he was surprised the whole platform wasn't swaying. He closed his eyes and prayed silently for God to give him the strength to see this through.

He heard an impatient voice from behind him. "Let's get goin' already."

He opened his eyes, turned, and noticed a man with bloodshot eyes leaning against the wooden frame by the lever, sipping from a flask. Several of the officers looked at the man in disgust. The man swayed slightly, obviously intoxicated.

"What?" the drunk man asked, looking from face to face. "The people came for a show. It's time to give 'em what they want," he slurred before wiping his nose on the back of his hand and spitting off the edge of the scaffold.

The officers shuffled Daniel forward until he was standing directly on the white X that had been scrawled on the wood trap door with chalk. He turned to the left and raised his eyes to look at the bright yellow sun rising in the east above the rooftops. He decided right then that he wanted that bright sun to be the last thing he saw on this earth - the beautiful, early morning rays of sunlight peeking over the buildings. He breathed deeply of the fresh air. He recalled the verses Father Wheatley had read to him.

Yea, though I walk through the valley of the shadow of death…

A dark hood was slipped over his head, blocking out the sun. It came all the way down to his shoulders. The fabric felt heavy and thick and caused his cheeks to itch. He inhaled a damp, musty smell, as if it had spent years tucked away in a basement somewhere.

…I will fear no evil…

A leather belt was fastened around his ankles, another at his thighs, and a final strap was cinched tightly around his chest and arms, pinning them to his sides. The crowd was so quiet, he could hear the faint *chink, chink* of the metal buckles being fastened.

…I will fear no evil…

Beads of sweat popped out all over his body as his mind drew a blank. *What was the next part?* He had recited the scripture over and over until it was tattooed on his brain, and yet he could not recall the next words.

In a panic, he called out, "I want to speak with Father Wheatley!"

"What?" he heard someone ask, the voice muffled by the heavy hood covering his ears.

"I need to speak to Father Wheatley!"

What was next?

"I will fear no evil…"

And then what?

"There ain't no time for that now, boy," said the drunk man from his post by the lever.

Daniel nodded, his breath coming in ever quicker shallow gasps.

No time for that now. No time for anything. He would cling to what he remembered.

Sally's warm, brown eyes.

Her tender smile.

...I will fear no evil…

Someone slipped the heavy rope around his neck and adjusted it so the bulging knot rested just behind his left ear.

...I will fear no evil…

The rope was tightened until it pressed slightly against his throat, and suddenly he remembered.

...for thou art with me ...

CHAPTER FORTY-ONE - LILLIAN

August 14, 1936

"What's happening?" Lillian asked, panicked. The hood and rope had been put into position, the prisoner stepped forward onto the trap door, Mr. Jackson nodded, all had gone according to plan. And yet, the prisoner still stood on the scaffold, the officers still stood at their posts, and the crowd still stood silent, watching and waiting.

"I'm not sure, ma'am," Tompkins replied in a quiet voice, his eyes glued to the scene.

"My God! Why isn't he pulling the lever?" she knew her voice was becoming hysterical, but she could not seem to control it. The crowd, which had been silent and unmoving as if holding its collective breath, was now beginning to stir as confusion set in.

"I don't know. I don't know what's happening," Tompkins answered. "Why isn't he pulling the damn lever?"

Just then, they saw Jackson turn and wave his arms at Hunt, who stood frozen, his hand on the lever. Jackson stepped closer to him and yelled, "Do it!" His booming voice carried across the lot and seemed to echo off the walls of the surrounding buildings. The prisoner jerked slightly and tried to turn his head in their direction.

Hunt stood dumbfounded, his hands clutching the lever as if unsure of its purpose or why he was standing on this platform in front of thousands of people, like an actor struck with a horrible case of stage fright at the worst possible moment.

The officers standing on the platform looked from Hunt to Jackson and back again as the crowd's murmuring grew.

Lillian tore open the door and jumped out of the car. Her knees felt weak as she stood and her head was spinning, but she moved forward as if drawn by an invisible string. She had to be ready to run forward, to mount the scaffold, grasp the lever, and pull it herself if these men failed to complete their task. That was the plan. That had been the plan all along.

Jackson waved his arms at Hunt as if hoping to break the spell that had come over him him, but to no avail. His voice carried across the crowd as he yelled again, louder this time. "Do it now!" Still, Hunt simply stood there and stared wide-eyed back at him, as if frozen in place. He glanced from Jackson to the crowd, to the prisoner still standing there on the X, and back to Jackson, his head pivoting slowly on his shoulders.

Lillian felt her body being propelled towards the crowd. All eyes were locked on the platform above, so only one person noticed her striding towards the scaffold.

Deputy Mitchell, standing next to Father Wheatley, glanced over and locked eyes with Lillian. He quickly shook his head in her direction, pushed Hunt aside, and leaned over onto the lever, springing the trap.

CHAPTER FORTY-TWO - DANIEL

August 14, 1936

He heard the yelling.

He heard the confusion.

The seconds ticked by like hours.

And then, it was just one deep breath.

The loud snap of the trap door slamming open.

A split second of weightlessness.

A rush of wind.

Silence.

Blackness.

… *And I shall dwell in the house of the Lord forever.*

CHAPTER FORTY-THREE - SALLY

August 14, 1936

The lever was pressed and the door fell open with a loud crack that echoed across the top of the silent crowd. The sound seemed to pierce through the glass window like a bullet and hit her chest with a force that made her stumble backwards. She saw him disappear for a split second, only a fraction in time, the space on the scaffold now empty where he had stood, like some magic trick at a circus sideshow. And then, just as suddenly, he reappeared below the trap, abracadabra, his body a narrow, heavy weight swaying slightly. She felt herself swaying with him, and then falling and falling endlessly, as if his shrouded form was an anchor pulling her down into the depths with him, the loud snap of the door still echoing in her ears, blackness seeping in from the corners of her eyes, a silent scream forming on her raw lips until all that was left of her world was darkness and silence.

CHAPTER FORTY-FOUR- SARAH

July 8, 2006

"Sarah?"

I barely recognized her choked and ragged voice. In that brief moment, just before the panic set in, I remember wondering how strange it was that after thirty years, my mother's voice could suddenly sound so foreign to my ears.

"Sarah?" she said again, louder this time.

"Mama, I'm here. What's wrong?" The blood in my veins turned to ice, and a cold sweat broke out on my forehead.

"I need you to meet me at the hospital." Her voice broke. She took a raspy breath before continuing in a whisper. "It's your grandfather."

My keys were in my hand before she had even finished the sentence.

I don't remember the drive to the county hospital, but I do remember running through the doors to the ER. I remember the exact moment it happened, the instant I felt like I had slammed into an invisible brick wall as I found myself staring breathlessly into the eyes of a nurse - the same nurse who had been there when my world was shattered a few months before.

She noticed my frantic expression and asked, "Can I help you?" and I realized she had absolutely no idea who I was. How could she not know? How could she not remember Steve carrying me through these same doors that night? I looked down at her hands, one holding a chart and the other poised above the computer keyboard at her desk. How could she not remember what happened after, the quiet voices murmuring outside the door as if I couldn't hear them, how she had placed those very hands on mine, smiling a sad smile and telling me it was going to be okay, that I could somehow pick up the shattered pieces of my life and move on? How could she not remember the sobs I couldn't contain as we left that hospital without our baby, my arms as empty as my heart?

"Ma'am, can I help you?" she asked again, growing concern on her face.

My mind was a blank, and my tongue seemed glued to the roof of my mouth. I looked around at the worried faces all around the ER waiting room. Painful flashes came back to me, a barrage of memories I had worked hard to stuff down into the depths of my soul so that I would never have to face them again. The antiseptic smell, the florescent lights, the muffled beeps and hushed voices and television game shows with the sound turned down low, the light blue institutional paint colors designed to comfort and calm.

"Sarah?" I heard my mother's weepy voice from far away and turned to look down the hallway. She stood with her arms open wide, tears streaming down her face, and I ran to her. I ran away from the nurse, away from my painful memories, and toward my mother, collapsing against her.

No words were needed. I already knew. I was too late. He was gone.

CHAPTER FORTY-FIVE - SALLY

October 2, 1936

She had dreamed of this day, imagined this very moment for so long. And now, here it was. She was so close.

She smoothed down the collar of her blue dress. She had spent too much on this dress, but she needed to make a good impression. She had ironed it carefully, but it seemed that no matter how many times she pressed it this morning, the left collar would not lay flat. She hoped no one would notice, that the person doing the interview would be so impressed with her words that he wouldn't see her collar sticking up. Maybe he wouldn't know she felt as out of place as a daisy in a snowstorm.

She plucked at a stray thread trailing from a button on the cushion of her chair. She sat a little taller, reminding herself to keep her shoulders back, to appear confident, even if she didn't feel it on the inside. She willed her knees to stop shaking, her heart to slow its steadily increasing pace. She folded and unfolded her hands in her lap.

She began absently spinning the thin gold band on her left ring finger. She hadn't really been able to afford it, but the man in the small jewelry shop on Davis Street smiled sympathetically at her when she told him she needed an inexpensive wedding ring, that she somehow lost hers when doing the wash. She looked him right in the eye and explained that her husband had sent her with a small portion of their savings and told her to pick out any ring she wanted to replace it.

She learned that trick from her daddy. People would believe most anything if you just looked 'em straight in the eye.

"You look like you're here to ask about a job."

She snapped back to the present, her memories interrupted by a man sitting across the room. She had been so nervous, she hadn't even noticed him there. She smiled shyly and nodded her head. That was another trick she learned from her daddy. Sometimes, when you're in a tight spot, it's best to lay low and keep quiet.

"It's a good place to work, even if I do say so myself. And Lord knows good jobs are mighty hard to come by these days for folks like us," he said. "My name's Lance Johnson, by the way."

"Nice to meet you, Lance Johnson." She glanced at him. "I'm Sally."

"Sally? Well, that's my sister's name, too. Small world, huh?"

Sally laughed. "Yes indeed, it is." She cleared her throat.

"You got a last name, Miss Sally?"

"Of course," she said cooly, her guard up. He nodded, sensing the need to back off. He turned and picked up a magazine from the coffee table between them.

She found herself picking at the thread of her chair again and stealing glances at the handsome stranger sitting across from her. He turned the pages of the magazine slowly, and she watched him as he scanned each page from top to bottom, as if memorizing every picture, every word he saw there.

"So, you work here at the hotel?" The question was out of her mouth and hanging in the air between them before she had even realized she was going to ask it.

He looked at her and smiled. "Yes, ma'am. I used to shine shoes over at the Seelbach, but I've been shinin' here at the Brown for about four months now."

"I see."

He looked at her a moment, waiting, and then looked back down at the magazine.

"And do you like it here?" she asked.

His eyes slid back up to meet hers, and that impish grin formed again on his lips. "Yes, ma'am, I sure can't complain. The boss treats me pretty fair, and I make a decent wage. I never have a shortage of customers. Sure is plenty o' rich white folks with dirty shoes 'round here," he grinned.

She burst into laughter and covered her mouth delicately with one hand as he put the magazine back down on the table between them.

"Pardon me for askin', but do you have other young'uns, or is this gonna be your first?" He nodded his head at her swollen belly.

"No, this here is my first." She faltered a moment. "Our first."

She thought she saw something flicker in his eyes, but it was gone before she could be sure.

She sat up a little straighter and looked directly in his eyes. "My husband was killed in a train accident back home in Waverly, so I came here to make a fresh start."

He sat up and leaned forward slightly. "I am so sorry, Sally."

"Thank you."

"Do you have folks here in Louisville who are lookin' after you?"

"No, sir. My folks are both dead. I sold everything my husband and I had to pay my way here and help me get started on a new life."

Lance shook his head. "You're a brave woman, Sally, to come to a city like this all by yourself, and in your condition."

"I had to," she said. "There were too many memories and too much sadness back home. I had to get away." At least that part was true.

"I can imagine. How long were you and your husband married before it happened?"

She was caught off guard. She had not expected him to ask questions. She stared into his eyes. For some reason, she desperately wanted to tell this stranger the truth, to tell him that she had not been married to the baby's father. That she had made her way to Louisville after he died to try and make a new life for herself and her baby. That she was only seventeen years old. That this was not the life she had pictured for herself. That she wasn't brave at all. She was scared - more scared than she had ever been in her whole life. Every night, she would lie awake on the small cot in her room above the bakery on 4th Street and cry herself to sleep, terrified of the sounds of the city and the thought of raising this baby on her own.

She opened her mouth, but before she could answer, a smiling woman with short brown hair and kind eyes stood in the doorway and said, "Sally?"

"Yes, ma'am," Sally answered.

"Right this way. Mr. Kemper will see you now," the woman held the door open and gestured for Sally to follow.

As she stood to go, Lance walked towards Sally and extended his hand. "I hope to see you 'round, Miss Sally," he said. "Good luck to you." He bent and gently kissed her hand. She glanced towards the woman waiting in the doorway, but she seemed unaffected by Lance's gesture.

Looking back into Lance's kind eyes, she said, "Thank you. I hope to see you again, too." And she meant it.

CHAPTER FORTY-SIX - LILLIAN

November 3, 1936

Lillian sat down in the worn chair behind the desk, the same chair that her husband had sat in many times before. She could hear the others milling around in the hallway, anxious to hear the results. She had slipped into her office, and thankfully, no one seemed to notice. She needed a moment to herself. A moment to think.

She remembered the night Everett was elected sheriff. She had watched him celebrate right here in this office, with laughter and hugs and shots of bourbon all around. Eyes shining, he had winked at her from across the room, and she remembered thinking her heart would burst with pride.

She ran her fingers along the smooth wooden desk, then looked over at their framed wedding photo on the shelf, the only personal decoration Everett had ever placed in his office. He always said it wasn't really his office; it belonged to Waverly. And yet, she still felt him in this room, felt his presence from the moment she walked in each morning until the moment she closed the door for the last time each afternoon. To her, it didn't matter who wore the badge. This would always be his office.

She walked over to the shelf beside the desk and picked up the framed wedding photograph, running her fingers across the smooth glass. She stared at the smiling faces in the photo, so young and unaware of the hardships to come.

Have I made you proud, Everett? she whispered.

Just then, Judge Riney stepped through the doorway, waving a piece of paper in his hand. Her children came tumbling in after him, Mary's cheeks looking flushed and the boys jostling each other to be in front.

"Mother, it's done! It's done!" James said, breathless.

Lillian took a deep breath, nodded, and walked back to sit in the chair behind the desk before looking up at Judge Riney.

"And how does it stand?" she asked.

She gripped the arms of the chair, her knuckles turning white. She knew the citizens of Waverly had probably all expected her to step down when it came time for the election. She had certainly done an adequate job, but after all, she had only been appointed to fill her husband's position until a proper election could be held. No one expected her to actually run for sheriff; she had not even expected it herself. She was a housewife and mother - not a politician.

And yet, the officers had encouraged her to run, had reminded her of their admiration for her husband and their willingness to help her in any way they could, until she found herself agreeing to at least throw her name in the ring. Her children had accepted her new position and had all chipped in to make sure things at home ran smoothly while she was away. Most of all, she had realized to her surprise that she truly enjoyed the work. Her role as sheriff gave her a newfound purpose, an opportunity to make a difference in the community.

"Well, ma'am," Judge Riney smiled as he read from the paper in his hand, "it looks like you received 9,811 votes. Your two opponents, however, did not fair so well. Stephen Smith received two votes, and Tom Carter received only one!" Her boys whooped and hollered, Patrick and James running into the hall to share the good news. Judge Riney's smile turned into a bout of laughter when he saw her shocked expression as Patrick and Mary leaned in to squeeze her in a crushing hug.

She heard James shouting, "I knew it! I knew it!" from the hallway.

"What?" Lillian asked in a stupor. "Are you sure?"

"You heard him, ma'am," Deputy Mitchell said, grinning excitedly as he stepped into the office and came towards her. "You've won the election by a landslide. I'd say the people made their choice pretty clear!"

Mary grasped her hands. "Mother, I couldn't be prouder of you," she said, her eyes filling with tears. Patrick leaned in to give her a kiss on the cheek.

"Yes, this count surely leaves no room for doubt. You have done an outstanding job these past few months, Sheriff Conner, and I look forward to working with you for years to come," Judge Riney added.

"Thank you, Judge. And thank you, Mitchell. Lord knows I would not have made it this far without your help," she said, smiling up at him.

"We make a good team," he answered softly.

The judge cleared his throat, and she turned to shake his hand and thank him again. Mary, Patrick, and the officers slowly spilled out into the hallway. She looked up to see Mitchell still standing in the doorway watching her, a wide grin on his face.

"Congratulations again, Madam Sheriff, on officially being elected sheriff. I, for one, couldn't be more proud." She found herself giggling like a schoolgirl when he tipped his hat to her. With a wink, he turned to join the celebration that now spilled out into the street.

Lillian turned towards the window. She heard the loud cheers and calls of "Congratulations!" echoing from the hallway as the news spread, but she felt as if she were underwater, the sounds somehow muffled and distant. It was hard to believe those cheers were for her. Six months ago, she had been a simple housewife and mother whose husband had fallen ill. Since then, she had become a widow, a sheriff, and had overseen a public hanging, the first one ever conducted by a female sheriff in the United States. She had been interviewed by reporters from all over the country. Her picture had been in the New York Times.

She turned to look back at the old, wooden desk. She felt Everett's presence so strongly in that moment, she halfway expected to see him sitting in his chair, smiling and winking at her.

She suddenly remembered his words to her during the nerve-wracking days leading up to his own election three years earlier. "I just want to help people, Lillian.

That's all I want. Just a chance to help people and make a difference in Waverly."

Now, it was her turn.

CHAPTER FORTY-SEVEN- SARAH

June 1, 2007

"Are you sure you need to be doing this, honey? I don't want you straining yourself, and it is way too hot in here." Mamaglanced around the attic, frowning at fifty years worth of memories in towers of dusty boxes and plastic totes.

"I'm fine, Mother," I said, rolling my eyes. Steve winked at me over her shoulder and handed me a glass of lemonade.

"Well, I don't want you to do too much. The first trimester is the most important, you know." She slid another box across the attic floor.

"Mama, I'm fine. Really. If it gets to be too much, I'll take a break. I promise."

"Okay, okay, if you're sure."

I took another swig of the ice cold lemonade and turned to see Mamastill watching me.

"What? You want a sip?" I grinned and offered her the glass.

"Oh, no, no, dear. It's nothing," she said, but I noticed that worried frown had appeared again.

"Mama, what is it now?" I silently prayed for patience.

"Nothing, nothing. You just look a little pale. Are you sure you're okay up here?"

"Are you serious right now?" I turned to look at Steve, unable to hide my exasperation.

Steve stifled his chuckling with a short cough and then said, "Okay, you two, let's get back to it so we can be done."

"Yes, let's get this job done so Sarah can get out of this heat," Mamaanswered as she lifted the lid from a box and set it aside, releasing a puff of dust from the floor.

"I can't believe all the stuff they kept all these years. I mean, really, what are we supposed to do with all of these old papers?" She held up several yellowed pamphlets.

"Whoa, look!" Steve snatched them from her hand. "Those are ration books from World War II!"

"Wow, seriously?" I moved closer to get a better look. "That's pretty cool."

"I wonder what else is in here?" Steve began pulling stacks of old photographs, ancient magazines, and more yellowed papers from the box.

"These look like letters Dad wrote when he was fighting overseas," Mamasaid in a soft voice as she flipped through a stack of envelopes. "It looks like he wrote home every week, and your Granny Patsy must have kept every single one."

Steve peered into the box and removed a small flask in a leather pouch. He turned it over in his hands and traced the initials carved into the front of the smooth, worn leather. "These are your grandfather's initials, but why would he have a flask? I thought he didn't drink?"

"No, he never drank. Like, never ever touched a drop. Maybe someone didn't know that and gave it to him as a gift or something," I shrugged.

"Yeah, but why would he keep it? I mean, it was in this box with all of these keepsakes and special mementos. You'd think he would have tossed it or given it away a long time ago."

We both looked at Mama, who was staring at the flask.

"Mama, do you know why he would have something like this?"

I saw her take a breath and swallow before answering. "Well, you're right. He didn't drink when you knew him, but that's because of some trouble when he was a younger man. Your grandmother told me that he had been an alcoholic at one time, actually. He gave up drinking about the time he and your Granny Patsy got married, back in 1937, so he must've had that flask before then."

"What?" I asked, incredulous. "Why did I not know about this?"

"It wasn't something he was proud of, Sarah. Your grandfather had a lot of secrets. There were things he never talked about, and he had his reasons."

Steve and I waited in silence. She looked down, took another deep breath, and continued. "He's gone now, so I guess there's no harm in you knowing the truth. Your grandfather used to be different, Sarah. It's hard to explain."

"Mama, I need you to try," I said softly.

"Okay, you're right." She sat down on an ancient trunk, wiped her bangs back off her face, and began her story. "I remember when your grandfather caught me drinking behind the barn. I must've been about sixteen.

Karen had taken a bottle of bourbon from her dad's liquor cabinet and brought it over to our house. We were passing the bottle back and forth, giggling, you know, just having fun like kids do. Your grandfather must have heard us laughing. He came around the corner and..."

She closed her eyes, as if to shut out the memory. Steve and I waited, but she remained silent. She finally looked at Steve, and then at me, tears filling her eyes. "Sarah, I don't really want to talk about this right now," she said quietly.

"What? What do you mean, you don't want to talk about it?" Anger bubbled inside me and I felt my cheeks flush.

"It was a long time ago, Sarah, and it's not something I want to remember."

I felt as if I was going to explode. "What is wrong with this family?" I shouted. "You sound just like him! Why are you so worried about holding on to secrets? So he caught you drinking behind the barn. Big deal! What's so terrible that you can't talk about it?"

Steve came and put a hand on my shoulder. I looked at him, and he gave me a slight shake of the head. Exasperated, I turned to look back at Mamaand forced myself to take a deep breath before speaking.

"Mama, look, don't you know that whatever happened is a part of who you are, and that makes it a part of me?"

She sniffed and then wiped her nose with the back of her hand. "I just hate the thought of you finding out your Grandaddy wasn't who you thought he was."

"What do you mean?" I whispered.

"Sarah, honey, you never saw him get angry. I mean really angry. I don't think you understand how angry he was that day he caught me and Karen. I had never seen him like that. He came around the corner of the barn, and Karen took off running for home. He stood there and stared at me, and I remember feeling so ashamed. I opened my mouth to try and explain, try to come up with some excuse, but before I could say anything, he grabbed me by the arms and shook me until my teeth rattled. Then, he slapped me across the face again and again and threw me down on the ground." She reached one hand up and placed it gently against her cheek, as if she could still feel the sting of it after all these years. "He stood there over me, shouting the whole time. I've never seen him so angry. Your grandmother ran out of the house and pulled him away before he could put his hands on me again."

Steve and I sat listening in shocked silence. I simply could not wrap my head around it. Grandaddy had a short fuse and would occasionally lash out at Granny Patsy during an argument, but only with words. Never with his hands.

"Later that night," Mamacontinued, "I asked your Granny Patsy why he had been so angry with me. And she told me his secret. She said he battled alcohol as a young man and made some bad decisions that he was still paying for. She wouldn't tell me what, just said it was better to leave it in the past. She said he was horrified to think that I might be going down that same path, and he somehow lost control."

She scooted closer and took one of my hands in both of hers. "I know this is hard for you to hear, Sarah, and even harder to understand. But that was his greatest fear - that his children would become enslaved to alcohol the way he had been."

I shook my head in disbelief. Grandaddy had often preached about the dangers of drinking when I was growing up, and yet, I had never even questioned why he was so against it.

Mama breathed out slowly, and then reached into the box. "We never spoke about it after that day. Like Granny Patsy said, some things are just better left in the past."

"Did he ever do anything like that again?" I asked in a quiet voice. "Hurt you, I mean?"

"No, honey, never," she shook her head. "Daddy was a good, good man. He never laid a hand on me after that day, I swear."

I nodded and swallowed the lump in my throat, fighting back the tears that threatened to spill over. Steve gently rubbed my back, and I leaned against him.

Mama sighed and turned back to the box between us. She pulled out a large, brown leather folio. "Here, Steve, we need a distraction. See what's in this." She held it out as she reached into the box with her other hand and pulled out a folder of papers.

Steve undid the clasp of the leather folio and opened it to find a plain black cassette tape. I picked it up and turned it over.

"What is it?" Mamaasked.

"I'm not sure," I said. "It's some kind of cassette tape, but there's no label on it or anything."

"See if there's anything else in there with it."

Steve held the folio wide open and we both peered inside. "Nope, there's nothing else in here. I wonder what's on it?"

"Who knows?" Mamasaid. "Your grandfather had so many radio sets and tapes. He was always tinkering around with stuff like that. Let me see if I can find a tape player. There's probably one in here somewhere with all of this ham radio junk, although I highly doubt there's anything special on that tape." She moved to another corner and began looking through boxes of jumbled wires and headsets. "Heck, there may not be anything on it at all."

Steve and I continued sifting through the piles of paperwork in the box, when we suddenly heard Mama's voice. "Aha! Here we go!" She held out a dusty old cassette tape player.

We gathered around and plugged the tape player into an extension cord. I slid the tape in and pushed play.

We all held our breath, but there was only silence.

"See? What did I tell you? It's probably..."

She was interrupted by a muffled scratching sound coming from the tape player. Seconds later, Grandaddy's voice filled the attic.

PART 5

THE SECRET

CHAPTER FORTY-EIGHT - *JAMES*

If you're listenin' to this tape, Patsy, it means one of two things. Either I've decided to finally tell you the truth, or, more'n likely, it means I'm dead and gone. Either way, what you're 'bout to hear is somethin' I've kept from you since the summer of 1936. I know I told you some of what what happened that summer, but I just can't seem to get up the nerve to tell you what all I remember. Sometimes I feel like it's eatin' me up inside, but I can't stand the thought of hurtin' you. Maybe one day you'll hear this tape and understand the truth about the man you married. I just hope you can find it in your heart to forgive me.

My memory sure ain't what it used to be, but I do recall nearly ever moment of that summer of '36. It was one of the hottest summers on record. I had gone to Louisville in the fall of '35 to try and make a new life for myself, but I had no idea what I was getting into.

I never told you much 'bout my time in Louisville, other than I had a drinkin' problem when I lived there. To your credit, you let it be and never pressured me to talk about it. But to understand my secret, first you have to know what happened in Louisville.

It started out simple enough. I got lucky almost as soon as I got to Louisville and found a job as a groundskeeper at a big hospital for tuberculosis patients. Growin' up on a farm like I did, I knew a thing or two 'bout flowers and plants and such, so it wasn't too hard to impress folks in the city with my green thumb. Besides, the work was easy compared to farm chores, and I was happy to be making my own way. Before long, I had a nice little apartment and things were going just fine.

But then, things changed. I don't even know how it happened, really. I started hangin' out with some of the guys after work, playin' pool and throwin' darts at a bar over by Iroquois Park.

I didn't know much 'bout poker back then, but I'm a quick learner, and this guy I met, Tommy was his name, he gave me some pointers. We started going to this bar almost every night after work, playin' cards with whoever was there, and I started drinkin' more and more. Sometimes, I would wake up on the floor of the bedroom in my little apartment with no memory how I got there. A lot of nights, I would stay out 'til two or three in the mornin' and show up at work with my head achin' somethin' awful. I started slackin' more and more, showin' up late, cuttin' corners, and before long, I lost that job I had been so proud of. But by then, I didn't even care. I was hooked. I couldn't stay away from the bars, I couldn't stay away from the gamblin,' and I sure couldn't stay away from the booze.

I met a guy named Allen McDaniel one night at the bar. He was a real flashy fella and offered to help me out when I was runnin' a bit short on funds. I kept playin' cards, and somehow over the next few days, I ended up rackin' up a mountain of debt to him. It was like I couldn't stop, Patsy. I kept thinkin' one more time would be enough. One more time, and I'd win big. This would be the one - the big pay off. But night after night, my excitement turned to disappointment. My big pay out - the windfall, the one that would let me pay off my debt to McDaniel and get the hell outta that God-forsaken city and back home where I belonged - it never came.

Allen McDaniel kept demandin' that I pay him back, but you can't squeeze blood from a turnip. McDaniel had a lot of friends, and those friends started followin' me.

I'd see 'em standin' across the street from the bar, smokin' a cigarette and watchin' me. I got so paranoid that every little sound made me jump. It got to where I expected to find somebody waitin' for me in the hall every time I opened the door.

I had nothing to hold me in Louisville. The city was not what I thought it would be. I thought I could make something of myself there, but I missed the farm. I missed my old life. I had thought Waverly was too small a place for me, not somewhere I could make a life of my own, that I needed to get away and see the big city. But I learned right quick the temptations in the city were too much for me. I wasn't cut out for no kinda life like that.

One night, somebody at the bar told me they heard McDaniel say he was gonna kill me if he didn't get his money, and I didn't doubt for a second that he would.

I knew I would never be able to pay it all back. I felt like I was drownin', and there was nothin' I could do.

And McDaniel was watching me. Everyday, he was watching and waiting.

So, I left.

I thought I could just run home and forget all about Allen McDaniel, but I was wrong.

I got a letter from McDaniel one afternoon not long after I'd moved back to Waverly. It came to the post office from Louisville with "James Graham, Waverly, KY" scrawled on the envelope. I knew who it was from before my shaking hands could even rip open the envelope. It was short and to the point.

You really thought you could hide, Graham? You thought I'd forget? I never forget.

I crumpled the letter and threw it in the trash can on my way out of the post office. I went to the bar on 5th, across from the park. I didn't have much money in my pocket. I got paid the week before for helpin' till the south field on the Woosley farm, but it wasn't enough. It would never be enough.

About an hour later, I left the bar and started walkin' down the street to the room where I had been stayin', tryin' to work out a plan in my mind. The whiskey hadn't done nothin' to clear my head, though my hands weren't shakin' no more, at least. I had learned that if I went too long without a drink, my body had a mind of its own. My hands would shake, my thinkin' was clouded, my breathin' too fast. The only thing that seemed to stop the shakin' was if I had another drink to steady my nerves.

I knew there was no point in tryin' to stay in Waverly any longer. If McDaniel knew I was there, it would take no time at all for him to send some of his men to take care of things. I was surprised he hadn't already done it, to tell ya the truth. And if he tracked me from Louisville to Waverly, he could track me from Waverly to anywhere. He had connections all the way from Chicago to Birmingham, and everywhere in between.

I kept on walkin' down the street, and I saw somebody stumble out of Tieggs' Tavern, the bar for coloreds down the street. He stood there a moment, as if strugglin' to gain his balance. A young colored girl stepped out of the tavern and spoke quietly to him. He bent to give her a kiss, and then she went back inside. He looked down the street, first one way and then the other, like he was tryin' to decide which way to go.

When he saw me, he put his head down and said, "Evenin', sir."

I nodded my head and started walkin' on by him, when suddenly, it dawned on me. I stopped and turned. "Say, are you that boy that broke into the Andersons' place awhile back?"

He looked up at me and seemed right scared for a minute, but then he just looked back down without sayin' anything.

"You must be the one. You look just like him," I said, steppin' closer to get a better look at him.

He glanced around before sayin', "Well, now, you see, sir, that was all a simple misunderstandin'."

"Yes, I'm sure it was. That's a shame," I said.

He tilted his head and looked up at me, surprised at my words.

"You served some time for that, didn't ya? I recollect seein' your picture in the paper."

"Yessir, I did. Just got out, matter o' fact." He kept puttin' his hands in and out of his pockets, as if unsure what to do with them.

I looked down at my my feet and suddenly, I realized a plan was indeed formin' in my mind. This boy could help me. And maybe I could help him.

"Why'd you try to break into their place, anyway?"

"Well, like I said, it was all a misunderstandin'. I was just lookin' to see if Mr. Anderson needed any more help. See, I'd did some work for him before. Matter o' fact, he paid me pretty good for helpin' him put a new porch on their house awhile back, and I was in desperate need of some money at the time. I'm tryin' to make my way back home to my sister's place near Roanoke."

"I see." The wheels of my mind started turnin'. I certainly knew all about how desperate a need for money could make you.

I looked at him a moment before decidin' it was worth a gamble. "So, are you still lookin' to make some real money?"

He looked up and met my gaze. His eyes searched mine and he seemed to think very carefully before answerin'. "Well, now, I reckon I'm always lookin,' sir," he said slowly.

"Well, maybe we can help each other out," I shrugged. I held my breath as I waited for his answer.

He looked at me for just a minute like he didn't know what to say before breakin' into a slow grin. "Well, sir, maybe we could. Can I ask who you are?"

I thought for a moment before I told him, "The only name you need to remember is Allen McDaniel."

I thought I was smart, Patsy. Oh, I thought I was so smart. I had a plan, and this was gonna solve all of my problems, once and for all.

But then, when it was all over, all I could think was, *What have we done? What have we done? What ... have... we... done?*

God as my witness, Patsy, it wasn't supposed to happen like that. I never in a million years could have imagined things would turn out like they did. I wish with all my soul I could go back to that night in April of '36 and just keep walkin' down the sidewalk.

The "what ifs" are enough to kill a man. *What if I had never gone to Louisville? What if I had never started drinkin'? What if I had not gone to the bar that night? What if I had kept walkin' past Daniel Porter without speakin' a word to him?* Oh, I wish I had. I wish I had never met him, never even laid eyes on him.

We had it all planned out, you see. We went over it time and time again. We knew exactly what was goin' to happen. What was supposed to happen. How could we have known the old lady would wake up?

It all started when Daniel dropped an iron on his foot that mornin'. He was always ironin' his clothes, trying to make sure every damn wrinkle was out. I never knew a negro who was as concerned about his appearance as Daniel Porter. It was like he always had somethin' to prove, like ironin' his shirt and makin' sure his shoes were clean would help people forget the sins of his past. He was always so worried about appearances. Hell, I don't know. Maybe he thought if he could make his clothes perfect, people would forget who he was. *What* he was.

We met that night in the alley, just like we'd planned. Some things from that summer are fuzzy, but this part, this part I remember clear as day. Daniel said he couldn't climb on account of his injured foot, so it would be up to me. That had never been part of the deal, but I looked at his foot, the shoe all cut open. Then, I looked up at the window above the alley and nodded my head.

I took my shoes off and left them against the building. I followed the path we had agreed on. First, up on the roof of the back porch of the building next door. Then, across the roof to the side. I held my breath as I made the short jump to the roof of the garage, hopin' the sound of my sock feet landin' on the tin roof wouldn't wake any curious neighbors. Then, up onto the roof of the side porch, across, and to the bedroom window. I glanced back at Daniel, and he looked both ways before lookin' up at me and noddin' his head.

So far, so good.

The window was open just a tad to let in what little breeze there was. I remember the nights were nearly as hot as the days that summer, even long after the sun had gone down. I slid the window up and climbed in, careful not to make a sound. Believe it or not, that was the easy part.

Once I was inside, I waited for my eyes to adjust to the darkness of the room. The moonlight was coming through just enough to let me see may way to the bedroom door. I also saw the old lady sleeping in her bed.

I crept through the house and downstairs to the back door, the moon shinin' through the windows and providin' my only light.

Daniel was waitin' at the back door lookin' nervous as a long-tailed cat in a room full o' rockin' chairs. I opened the door and let him in. He handed me my shoes, and I put them on and then followed him as he limped up the stairs.

My heart was poundin' somethin' fierce as I watched Daniel maneuver around the room. I shook my head to clear away the whiskey I had drank earlier to steel my nerves. I noticed a marble statue of a bird on the table by her bed. There was jewelry scattered in various ceramic dishes and boxes, just waitin' to be taken. I planned to sell my share and use it to pay off my gamblin' debts to Allen McDaniel, be free of him once and for all, and Daniel could take his part and make his way back home to Virginia.

Daniel was moving too slowly. He was examinin' each piece of jewelry, while I was openin' and closin' drawers, fillin' my pockets with as much as they would hold. Daniel picked up each piece as if determinin' its value before decidin' if he wanted to take it or not. I shook my head when I saw him remove his own black initial ring, place it on a table, and slide one of Mrs. Bower's rings down onto his delicate finger, like he was testin' the fit.

All of a sudden, I heard some rustlin' from the bed behind me. My heart near stopped as I turned and saw

Mrs. Bower sit up with a gasp. Wide-eyed, she looked straight at Daniel and cried out, "I know you!"

Right then, I reckon I stopped thinkin' and just started doin'. I couldn't let her wake the house. I knew she could scream at any moment, and there was no way we could explain our way out of this situation.

I never meant to hurt her, Patsy. Not really. I just needed her to be quiet.

In a split second, I grabbed the heavy bird statue from beside the bed. I don't remember swingin' it down, I don't remember hittin' her on the side of her head, but I do remember, to my everlastin' shame, that my first feelin' was not horror at what I had done, but relief. Relief that she was silent. Relief that she had never even seen me, standin' on the other side of the bed. She had only seen Daniel. Judge me if you must, sweetheart. The good Lord knows I have judged myself everyday since it happened.

I locked eyes with Daniel from across the room. He and I both knew that when she came to, she would be able to identify him as the one who had broken in. If she came to, that is. I looked back down at her and noticed a small trickle of blood near her ear, below where the statue had smashed into her temple.

I couldn't breathe. I felt like the the whole room was spinnin'.

What had I done? What had I done?

I don't remember what happened right after that. It's like there's a moment in time where I was standing there, lookin' at Daniel with the bed between us, and then my mind goes fuzzy and blank and dark for awhile.

The next thing I remember, I was runnin' down the middle of the street. I ran all the way home. I never looked back to see if Daniel was followin' me, or if he even made it out of that room.

I lived in fear as Daniel hid out and then was captured by the police. I shaved off my moustache and tried to only go out after dark, with a hat pulled down low on my forehead. I took the ferry across the river to Evanston a couple of days later and pawned the jewelry I had shoved in my pocket that night. I sent the money to Allen McDaniel in Louisville, thankful that he would no longer be after me, but wonderin' if I would still spend the rest of my days hidin'.

I expected the sheriff and her deputies to come knockin' on my door any time, maybe to even bring Daniel with them. I could picture his face, his finger pointin' at me. I could even hear him sayin' it.

He's the one. It was his idea all along.

I poured over every newspaper article about the case. And then one day, my heart just about stopped when

I read how Daniel Porter told police he had an accomplice. To my great relief, the reporter commented that the police said Allen McDaniel was probably just a figment of Porter's imagination, somethin' designed to distract the police.

You might wonder if I ever thought 'bout comin' clean, 'bout turnin' myself in, and the truth is, I did, I really did. I thought about it a lot, especially when I read about the verdict in the papers. But in the end, I was a coward. I couldn't own up to what I had done. Hell, I couldn't even remember much of anything after I hit her with that statue. But the guilt and shame I felt that day when Daniel was executed... well, it was enough to make me turn my life around and swear off drinkin' from there on out, and to this day, I haven't touched a drop.

Now you know why.

I was there, by the way, the day Daniel was hanged. I watched with a few other fellas from the rooftop of a restaurant over on Locust Street. It was the first time I'd seen Daniel since the night it happened. I watched him mount those steps, turn to face the crowd, and move to stand over the trap. Patsy, I could have swore he looked right at me right before they placed that black hood over his head and shoulders, but then I closed my eyes.

I couldn't bear to watch.

CHAPTER FORTY-NINE - SARAH

June 12, 2007

I stood looking down at the polished tombstone and the bouquet of white hydrangeas standing in the vase next to his name, carved in heavy block letters. *James Darrell Graham. March 3, 1916 - July 8, 2006 - Husband and Father.*

I realized, after everything that had happened, how true it is that we all wear masks, how most people never get to see us without our defenses up. Still, I felt as if my world had been turned completely upside down. This man that helped raise me, the man who dried my countless tears, slipped me an extra cookie when Mamawasn't looking, the one who taught me to fish. He kept a dark secret for so many years, a secret that could have changed the outcome of Daniel Porter's trial. Oh, sure, Daniel would probably have still been found guilty. A black man in the segregated south in 1936 wouldn't have much of a chance if found guilty of raping a white woman. But still. If the jury had known that he did not act alone, that someone else had been there, had struck the first, and perhaps fatal, blow, things could have turned out very differently.

And what if the story my grandfather recorded on that tape was not the whole truth? He even said his memory was fuzzy in some places, that he couldn't exactly remember certain details. He admitted being out of control, that he had a habit of drinking until he would pass out. I thought I knew him, knew what he was capable of, but I was obviously wrong. In an era before DNA testing, was there any way to prove without a doubt who had actually raped and killed Suzanne Bower? I shuddered.

No one could ever definitively know what had happened that night. Daniel's ring found at the crime scene was the only evidence to tie him directly to the crime, but it was circumstantial at best. I knew that given the time period, his confession may very well have been given under duress.

He had been convicted and executed on the basis of those two things alone - a ring and a possibly false confession.

Daniel Porter implicated an Allen McDaniel more than once when speaking to the police, though I could find no record of what exactly Daniel claimed his involvement was in the crime. Regardless, the police searched and tried to find Allen McDaniel but were unsuccessful.

It was almost too much to take in.

I walked up the hill, one hand on my aching back, and followed the path to the back of the cemetery, the area known for years simply as "Potter's Field." It was marked with plain wooden crosses and a few smaller tombstones, as well as vast patches of open grass with no markers at all. There were no large monuments, no vases of flowers, no ancient statuesque tombstones to honor lost loved ones in this section. This was where the city had buried paupers for years, those without relatives or means to pay for a burial plot and headstone. This was where people were buried and forgotten.

According to the newspapers, Daniel had asked that his body be sent to his family in Virginia for burial, but his request was ignored. The city wasn't about to spend any extra money to transport his body, after the expenses incurred by the investigation, trial, and subsequent execution. Instead, he was brought here.

I walked along the rows until I came to an empty grassy area near a large oak tree. Daniel's unmarked grave was supposedly somewhere in this area. I scanned the patch of grass, taking in the clover that covered the area, and tried to find some indication of where his grave might be.

I wondered what Daniel's sister had heard about the crime and the trial. I could find no record of his sister ever visiting him in jail or even contacting him at all. Was she surprised by the way things turned out, or had she always known her little brother would come to no good end?

I turned and looked down over the grassy hill at the sea of tombstones, and realized I could see my grandfather's grave from this vantage point. How ironic, that these two men, brought together under dangerous and horrific circumstances, now found their final resting places mere steps away from one another. Two men, whose lives were so different. One was a respected farmer who left a family and legacy to be proud of, buried with a regal gravestone worthy of honoring his life. The other, a young black man who faced adversity everyday of his life, buried in an unmarked grave to be forgotten. And yet, they were tied together, as if an invisible line stretched across the grass between their graves, connecting them in a way no one would ever know.

I walked slowly back to the car and drove home with the air conditioning turned off, feeling chilled, despite the summer heat. Steve wasn't home from work yet, so I let myself in the house, poured a glass of sweet tea, and sat at my desk.

I thought about all that had happened in the past year, and all that I had learned about my grandfather - the man I thought I knew, and the man he really was.

I took my grandfather's tape out of my desk drawer and held it in my hands. I thought back to that day in the attic, the day my mother, my husband, and I sat listening, in awestruck wonder. We had been faced with a choice regarding our family's secret that day. We could stay silent and keep the secret, or we could tell the world the truth, no matter how painful it would be. The whole truth. The truth about how my grandfather had played a pivotal role in the horrific crime leading to the last public execution that took place on American soil. The truth about our family's secret.

I took a yellow pencil out of the desk drawer and slid it under the ribbon of tape. I pulled gently until a slick loop was protruding from its plastic shell. And then, I grabbed the loop and pulled with my fingers, unraveling the ribbon of tape into a pile on my desk. I pulled until there was nothing left in the plastic shell and a huge, tangled jumble of glossy tape was sitting in front of me. I picked up the scissors and began cutting. I looked down at my swollen stomach, thinking of the child within that would grow up never knowing how her great-grandfather had been involved in a murder. A child that would never have to worry about someone finding out about her family's secrets.

After all, it's like my Grandaddy always said. Some things are just better left in the past.

AUTHOR'S NOTE

Waverly began with a story idea based on events surrounding the last public execution in America, which just so happened to be in the town where I live. That basic idea bounced around in my head for several years until a manic writing spree one summer in which I consumed massive amounts of iced coffee on my patio in the early morning hours and wrote an entire 60,000+ word manuscript in thirty days.

From there, the book required more time, energy, and revisions than I could have ever imagined. The funny thing is, the finished product bears little resemblance to my original plan. I changed plotlines, character names, and even the title.

Writing a novel is a lot like navigating around a new city without a map. You have a vague idea of where you're going and the basic skills to get there, but who knows what detours and distractions you'll find along the way?

When I first began, I wanted to write a nonfiction account of the events as they actually happened. I spent hours researching at the public library and online, gathering photos, articles, and various documents. I combed through newspaper accounts, published interviews, the trial transcript, and a fascinating work called *The Last Public Execution in America* by Perry Ryan.

The scene where Sarah visits the Kentucky Room and feeds multiple coins into the machines to print out articles from microfiche? Yeah, that was based on my own experience researching for this book.

After all, what was the point in changing anything? The true story was so fascinating, it was like a ready-made novel. I felt it was almost too easy. All I had to do was simply record the events as they happened. It already had the makings of a great plot - a vicious crime, a tense manhunt, a dramatic trial, a female sheriff in charge of overseeing a public execution, a media frenzy with thousands of spectators, even a drunk hangman failing to pull the trapdoor lever at the appointed time. Why mess with such an amazing story?

But as I threw myself into the research, I realized this was more than just a suspenseful, edge of your seat story. This was a story of real people whose lives were forever changed by the events. It's the story of a town haunted to this day by what happened here back in 1936.

I love my town. I love the people here, and I love the history of this place, even though some parts left wounds that were slow to heal. Many descendants of those involved would rather forget about this blight on our town's history. That is why, early on in this project, I decided to give myself the freedom of fictionalizing some parts of the story and telling it my way.

In spite of this, many of the elements that are central to the crime scene, investigation, trial, and execution are based on actual events that occurred in Owensboro, Kentucky in the summer of 1936.

The criminal, whose real name was Rainey Bethea, really did enter the crime scene through an upstairs window, leave his ring on the table, and steal jewelry and a white dress with bright, orange flowers from the victim.

Bethea really did change into a clean pair of socks as he climbed the stairs to the gallows. This little fact was oddly fascinating to me, so I decided to invent Daniel's obsession with keeping his appearance neat to account for it.

Other facts I chose to include in *Waverly* are that the sheriff really did take over after her husband died of pneumonia, Bethea hid out for three days before being captured, and there were in fact some who questioned whether Bethea's confessions were coerced. Bethea entered a guilty plea to the charge of rape, and the jury returned a sentence of death by hanging after deliberating for only five minutes.

The female sheriff, Florence Thompson, really did win the official election after her appointment by the judge by an overwhelming majority. Her two opponents received a combined total of 3 votes.

I came across a statement by a twelve-year old witness in the trial transcripts who stated he saw Bethea the day of the murder and talked to him about a foot injury. This was what really sparked the mystery for me. What if Rainey Bethea had an accomplice? What if the there was more to the story?

From there, the completely fictional characters of James Graham (and, subsequently, Allen McDaniel and Sally Davidson) were born, and all intentions I had of writing a nonfiction, fact-based account flew out the window. The resulting novel you now hold in your hands is a hybrid of my town's infamous history and my own imagination - a story rooted in the truth, but steeped in a whole lot of "what ifs."

Amy Bellamy

January 2019